He could have sworn that when he first kissed her, she'd almost opened up to him, at least physically.

Then she'd stalked off without a word. Banged down the shutters in his face. And but for an occasional brief, unwitting chink, she'd kept them down ever since.

If she thought he'd back off, she could think again. She'd thrown out a challenge, and he'd never refused one in his life. One day he'd make her acknowledge that this unsettling desire to touch, to explore, to *know,* wasn't all on his side.

She might be the boss's daughter, heiress to Kingsley's little kingdom, but she'd learn that sex was the great leveler. When it came down to it, a naked princess was like any other woman without her clothes....

Dear Reader,

Calling all royal watchers! This month, Silhouette Romance's Carolyn Zane kicks off our exciting new series, ROYALLY WED: THE MISSING HEIR, with the gem *Of Royal Blood*. Fans of last year's ROYALLY WED series will love this thrilling four-book adventure, filled with twists and turns—and of course, plenty of love and romance. Blue bloods and commoners alike will also enjoy Laurey Bright's newest addition to her VIRGIN BRIDES thematic series, *The Heiress Bride*, about a woman who agrees to marry to protect the empire that is rightfully hers.

This month is also filled with earth-shattering secrets! First, award-winning author Sharon De Vita serves up a whopper in her latest SADDLE FALLS title, *Anything for Her Family*. Natalie McMahon is much more than the twin boys' nanny— she's their mother! And in Karen Rose Smith's *A Husband in Her Eyes*, the heroine has her eyesight restored, only to have haunting visions of a man and child. Can she bring love and happiness back into their lives?

Everyone likes surprises, right? Well, in Susan Meier's *Married Right Away*, the heroine certainly gives her boss the shock of his life—she's having his baby! And Love Inspired author Cynthia Rutledge makes her Silhouette Romance debut with her modern-day Cinderella story, *Trish's Not-So-Little Secret*, about "Fatty Patty" who comes back to her hometown a beautiful swan—and a single mom with a jaw-dropping secret!

We hope this month that you feel like a princess and enjoy the royal treats we have for you from Silhouette Romance.

Happy reading!

Mary-Theresa Hussey

Mary-Theresa Hussey
Senior Editor

The Heiress Bride

LAUREY BRIGHT

SILHOUETTE *Romance*®

Published by Silhouette Books

America's Publisher of Contemporary Romance

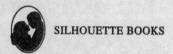

SILHOUETTE BOOKS

ISBN 0-373-19578-8

THE HEIRESS BRIDE

Copyright © 2002 by Daphne Clair de Jong

This edition published by arrangement with Harlequin Books S.A.

Visit Silhouette at www.eHarlequin.com

Printed in U.S.A.

LAUREY BRIGHT

has held a number of different jobs, but has never wanted to be anything but a writer. She lives in New Zealand, where she creates the stories of contemporary people in love that have won her a following all over the world. Visit her at her Web site, http://www.laureybright.com.

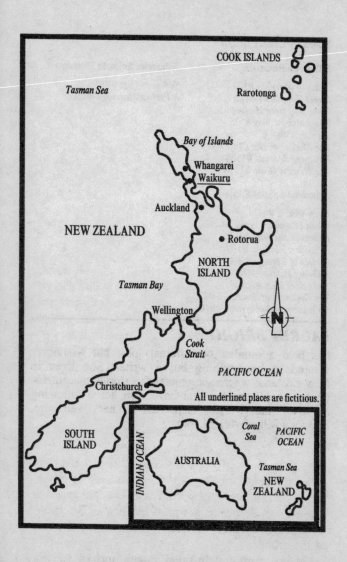

COOK ISLANDS

Tasman Sea

Rarotonga

Bay of Islands

● Whangarei
Waikuru

Auckland ● ●

● Rotorua

NEW ZEALAND

NORTH
ISLAND

Tasman Bay

Wellington ●

*Cook
Strait*

PACIFIC OCEAN

All underlined places are fictitious.

Christchurch ●

N

SOUTH
ISLAND

INDIAN OCEAN

*Coral
Sea*

PACIFIC
OCEAN

AUSTRALIA

Tasman Sea

NEW
ZEALAND

Chapter One

It was a humid summer evening, and the annual *Waikura Clarion* Christmas party was in full swing.

Checking that the guests were enjoying themselves, Alysia paused in the doorway of the big front lounge.

Her father, wine glass in hand, held forth to a respectful circle of his employees. Spencer Kingsley was a big man, and his confident stance, rich baritone voice and command of language ensured that people listened to him.

Only one person had let his attention stray; Chase Osborne, the chief reporter, stared absently into his glass.

As Alysia stood watching, Chase raised his dark head and looked directly at her with unblinking green-brown eyes under emphatic black brows. He gave her a courteous nod, then his gaze left her as her father threw back his head in laughter, echoed by the rest of the group.

Chase's firmly delineated mouth moved only a

fraction of an inch at one corner before he downed the remainder of his drink.

He had scarcely noticed Alysia, despite the green chiffon designer dress that exposed the smooth skin of her arms and shoulders, complemented her fine, fair hair, and emphasized eyes the same clear light green as the pendants in her ears, carved from translucent New Zealand inanga jade.

Her eyes were her best feature, though when she was younger she'd thought green a wishy-washy color, longing for a more positive blue or brown.

Once she had horrified her father by using a strawberry rinse in her hair. Now she occasionally had her hairdresser use highlights in the winter to give it a bit of life.

She was no great beauty, but tonight several people had commented favorably on her appearance, and even her father had said that she'd never looked prettier, lighting a tiny glow inside her.

For Chase Osborne she might have been just another piece of furniture in the crowded room.

"Allie!" A rotund middle-aged man appeared at her elbow. The *Clarion's* advertising manager, Howard Franklin was one of the few people who habitually shortened her name. "You've done a great job."

"Thank you, Howard." She actually had done very little. Her father had told her which catering firm to hire and given her a list of staff members to invite. "I hope you and Mollie are enjoying yourselves."

Everyone seemed to be having a wonderful time. The younger contingent had gravitated from the swimming pool to the games room. Several couples were dancing on the terrace to music from a tape player, while older staff and their partners gathered in the lounge.

"Great, great," Howard assured her. "But you don't have a drink. Busy looking after everyone else, eh? Let me get one for you." He took her arm to guide her toward the bottles and glasses on a table in a corner.

A burly man with a flushed face turned from it as they approached, two frothing beer mugs in his hands. Verne Hastie was the print room manager. "Allie!" he said in overhearty tones. "Long time no see. All grown up, too!" Bold blue eyes approved the shoe-string-strapped dress and fitted bodice.

Alysia stiffened as her cool gaze briefly met his.

Verne grinned widely at Howard. "How come you're with the prettiest girl in the room, an old fogy like you?" he demanded. He laughed uproariously.

"I'm just getting Alysia a drink," Howard said. "What would you like, Allie?"

She turned to him with relief as Verne went off across the room. "Gin with lemon bitters. Make it strong."

Howard chuckled. "Well, you've had your twenty-first birthday." He poured the drink and handed it to her. "Here you are."

She gripped the glass tightly in a damp hand and took a generous gulp from it. Sweeping a glance around the room, she encountered Chase Osborne's dark eyes again. This time they were alert, his gaze dropping, apparently to gauge the level of the liquid in her glass before rising again to hers, curiosity and something that might have been a hint of concern stirring in his eyes.

A spoon tinkling against a glass brought Alysia's

attention to her father, who was standing near Chase. Someone killed the tape player and the dancers gathered at the French doors leading to the terrace, while other people were summoned from the games room.

Spencer cleared his throat. "Christmas being a family occasion, and you all being part of the *Clarion* family, this seems an appropriate time to make an announcement."

As Spencer's proud gaze traveled around the room Alysia felt a surprised thrill. She hadn't expected a formal announcement, though everyone probably knew already she was about to start working with them, her very first real job after leaving university.

Spencer smiled and continued. "As I'm getting on in years—" he paused for muted laughter and murmured denials around the room "—it's time I started thinking about the future. Young blood is always good for an old business and the *Clarion* is no exception. I've decided, therefore, to appoint a deputy editor."

Deputy? Alysia felt dizzy. Not a junior position in the newsroom after all. Instead a new position created just for her.

The business degree she'd taken before attending journalism school might have made her father think she'd be more valuable in management. But she'd expected to work her way up, not be presented with a plum position working at his side.

Flushing with embarrassed excitement, she took a step forward.

"So..." Spencer raised his glass. "Please drink to my right-hand man and the *Clarion's* deputy editor."

He turned to Chase and put an arm around his

shoulders. "Chase—here's to your new position. Congratulations."

All the blood drained from Alysia's cheeks. She felt herself go pale and cold, her temples thudding.

Everyone was raising their glasses, calling out their congratulations, and a smattering of applause broke out. Thank God no one was taking any notice of her. What a fool she'd almost made of herself.

Chase was smiling as Spencer shook his hand. "Thank you all very much," he said. "And Spencer, I'm deeply honored by your confidence in me."

Sycophant. Toady! A sour taste rose in Alysia's throat, almost choking her. While everyone else surged around the two men, offering Chase congratulations, she left the room, almost running along the wide passageway to a door that opened onto the old back veranda and the garden. She had to get away before anyone saw how upset she was. How betrayed she felt.

Quickly she descended the broad steps and crossed the moonlit lawn bordered by a mixture of native New Zealand evergreens and exotic hibiscus, roses and lavender. The trailing leaves of the pepper tree whipped at her face, startling her, and she breathed in their sharp scent as she went on.

Beyond the formal garden a path wound between thick shrubs, and at its end a low stone wall served the double function of retaining the steep bank and providing a place to sit and survey the view.

A sea of lights spread out far below, a winding curve of blackness marking the river that bisected the town. And beyond the farthest lights a range of hills created another black uneven line below the five stars of the Southern Cross and the pale misty swathe of the Milky Way.

Alysia sat on the wall, half turned to stare unseeingly at the winking of the lights imitating the crowded night sky overhead.

Gradually the turmoil inside her subsided, while she castigated herself for being such a fool. It didn't mean her father didn't love her...only that she was too young and inexperienced for a senior position and he knew it. *She* knew it. Her sickening disappointment was based on a fleeting false impression. She would just have to get over it.

Once she did start work she'd show him, show everyone—she'd be the best damned reporter the *Clarion* had ever had. Better even than Chase Osborne. And in a few years she'd be given her rightful place as the heir to the Kingsley heritage. Because she'd have earned it.

She stayed unmoving for a long time, scarcely hearing the revelry from the house, until the breeze wafting uphill from the river rustling and rattling the manuka and flax and occasional tall, lacy ponga fern covering the slope, made her shiver.

Rubbing at her bare arms, she got up, stopping with a small gasp as she saw the dark bulk of a man standing rock-still a few feet away.

"I didn't mean to scare you," Chase Osborne said.

"How long have you been there?" Her tone was sharper than she'd meant it to be.

Perhaps that was why he didn't answer straight away. "Your father sent me to find you."

It didn't answer her question, but after a half second's reflection she decided not to pursue it. "How did you know where to look?"

"It took me a while." He paused. "Are you all right?"

"Why shouldn't I be?" He hadn't guessed, had he, how nearly she'd invited humiliation? Her cheeks burned and she was thankful for the dim light.

Chase said, "You seemed to be knocking back your drink in there as if you needed a fix."

"I can handle my liquor. It was one glass of gin and lemon and I didn't even finish it." Or had she? She couldn't remember now what she'd done with it in her blind need to escape. Anyway, she was an adult. How much she drank needn't concern him. "I'm fine," she asserted.

She had an uneasy feeling he didn't believe her, but after a moment's silence he changed the subject. "This is quite a sight, isn't it?" He came to her side, looking down at the lights and the invisible river. The sleeve of his jacket brushed her arm, and she involuntarily flinched away.

Chase turned his head, and even in the dark she sensed his air of amused curiosity before he switched his attention back to the view.

"You must have seen it before," Alysia said.

"Never at night. Kingsley's kingdom."

Something in his tone made her defensive. "It's only a town."

He turned to her again. "Your family's town."

"We don't own it. Not anymore."

"In your great-great-grandfather's day—"

"That was a long time ago." Jasper Kingsley, only weeks off an immigrant ship from England, had bought land from the local Maori tribe, milled the standing timber that covered it, raised a settlement on the banks of the river—in those days a navigable water-way—and leased the cleared land to small farmers, making himself a sort of unofficial squire. He'd built the big house, at that time the only house on the hillside, from which he could survey his creation. But in over a century and a half the town had grown and times had changed.

"All we own now is the house and the newspaper," Alysia pointed out. "And a few old buildings," she added punctiliously. Plus various stocks and shares.

"Those old buildings are on prime sites," Chase reminded her. "Worth quite a lot in today's market."

She had no doubt he was right. Not that it was any of his business.

His voice butter-smooth, he added, "And one day they'll all be yours."

"I hope that day is a long way off," she told him tightly. And hoped he understood that she found discussing her father's death—even indirectly and only in theory—distasteful.

Chase turned, altering his stance so that he appeared to loom over her. He was blocking her way to the path. When she stepped forward he didn't budge.

Alysia raised her eyes to his face, half-lit by the blue-white moonlight. She'd never thought him a particularly good-looking man—his strong features were too well-defined, the bone structure too obvious. But he was striking, and close-up he presented a formidable air of masculinity.

She didn't recall that they had ever been alone before, unless she counted occasions when he had come to the house and she'd let him in to her father's study.

She smelled a faint aroma of clean clothing, soap and an underlying pleasant tang that reminded her of the sea. Aftershave? As he looked down at her the planes of his face seemed angular, the chin jutting and the straight black brows almost merged in a frown.

The noise of the party suddenly seemed very distant. The moon slipped behind a high cloud, deepening the darkness.

Alysia stepped back and felt her legs touch the wall. "By the way, congratulations." She hoped her voice sounded casual.

"Thank you. Do I get the feeling you aren't thrilled about my promotion?"

"What my father does at the *Clarion*, whom he appoints, is entirely up to him…at least for some years yet."

There was a telling silence while he absorbed the subtle warning. Then Chase enquired smoothly, "Looking to the future, are you? To when your father retires?"

"Are *you*?"

They remained staring at each other, the gloom making it difficult for her to see his expression.

Chase said, "I'm not a Kingsley."

"You needn't worry about your job yet." It would be years before she was ready to take over the business. Embarrassment at her brief earlier assumption crawled in her stomach.

"Did I say I was worried?" Chase sounded confident, amused. As though he saw her as a puny threat, at best.

"By the time my father retires I'm sure you'll have found yourself some wider, greener pastures. I promise I won't hold you back."

He rocked a little on his heels, his head slanted to

one side, hands sliding into his pockets. "You won't?" he said very softly. She knew he meant: *You think you could?*

Alysia's chest felt constricted, her cheeks hot. "You're ambitious," she said. "My father may think you'll stick around out of loyalty to him, but…"

"What do *you* think?" he challenged her. His voice deepening, he added, "Are you telling me this town isn't big enough for both of us?"

"Is it big enough for you?" She'd never thought so. Surely this job with a provincial, family-owned paper, however respected and prosperous, was a mere stepping stone in his career path.

He said, "That depends."

"My father won't give up control for a long while yet. It's always been a family concern."

"And you're the last of the family."

Alysia discovered that her hands were clenched. She loosened her fingers, flexed them secretly. "Within the next five, ten years…"

"You think you'll be ready to take over?" Chase queried.

Alysia's teeth hurt, and the incipient headache that had begun with her father's announcement had become an insistent throbbing. She hadn't meant to go so far. But if Chase Osborne imagined he was in line for editor-in-chief, a title that had always remained in family hands, it was time someone disillusioned him. It had only been fair to spell it out. She took in a quick breath. "If my father wants me, hadn't we better—"

Chase interrupted. "I didn't say he wanted you."

Her discomfort with his dark presence crystallized

into a jagged antagonism. Her chin lifted. "You told me—"

"That he sent me to find you," Chase said. "He wondered where you'd got to."

"Well, you've found me. Now either go back and tell him I'm here and I'm fine, or get out of my way."

He made no attempt to do so. "All in good time, Princess," he said lazily. "I'm not your lackey."

Unaccountably Alysia's heart was hammering. He hadn't moved an inch, but she sensed anger behind the deceptively gentle tone. An irrational, atavistic fear made her lash out with words. "No," she said, her head lifting to an unconsciously arrogant tilt. "You're my father's."

He seemed to be contemplating her, holding himself so still it was uncanny. The moon reappeared, throwing a faint nimbus around his head but scarcely lighting his face except for the glitter of his eyes. He made a short, sharp sound that might have been the beginning of a laugh. "Is that what you think?" he asked her. "He's my employer."

"So you jump when he says 'Jump' and obediently check up on his daughter when he tells you to. I didn't know that was part of the *deputy editor's* job description."

"It's part of being a guest in Spencer's house," Chase replied. "He didn't like to leave the party, as he's the host. I take it you didn't want to be found."

Ignoring the implication that she was neglecting her duties as her father's hostess, Alysia said, "I didn't *need* to be found! I would have been coming back in a minute anyway."

"Well, then—" at last he moved aside so that she could precede him "—I'll escort you."

She swept past him, and Chase followed, not speaking again. But she could feel his gaze like a burning laser right between her shoulder blades.

When they reached the pepper tree he stepped forward and lifted the hanging branch. As she passed under it a cool, spice-scented leaf brushed her cheek. Her bare shoulder came in contact with the fabric of Chase's jacket.

The house, lit from end to end, was before them, but they were still in the shadow of the tree when he caught her arm, drawing her back to face him.

Surprised, Alysia raised her head. "What is it?"

"Just this," he answered.

His hand slid about her waist, pulling her against him so that her body curved at the hard bar of his arm, and her head fell back in astonishment before his mouth descended on hers.

He ignored her startled movement, one hand going to her nape while his mouth continued to explore hers in a kiss that was surely too expert.

Too surprised at first to resist, she had let her lips remain soft under his, but now she closed them firmly against the seductive coaxing that invited her to reciprocate. She made herself rigid in his embrace, her hands splayed on his upper arms, feeling the tensing of the muscles when he tightened his hold. As his mouth insisted on a response from her, she counted to ten and refused to give in to the growing urge to kiss him back.

His fingers tangled in her hair and his lips compelled hers apart—until Alysia sank her teeth briefly and quite hard into his lower lip. She heard him give a low grunt deep in his throat before he raised his head and she was free.

Her high heels sinking in to the yielding turf beside the path, she nearly overbalanced. Chase grabbed at her wrist, half holding her off and half supporting her, and as she recovered herself she saw that he was silently laughing. He touched a finger gingerly to his lip and said, ''Not quite what I expected.''

''What did you expect, then?'' she asked, her voice low but shaking with anger and a peculiar sense of excitement. He surely hadn't thought she'd capitulate?

''What you tried at first,'' he said frankly. ''The stone statue impersonation. It was quite effective, too. But this—'' he touched his lip again ''—is...interesting.''

His tone held a kind of speculative respect.

He hadn't hurt her. But beneath the experienced technique that had forced her to fight her own arousal, the kiss had been an expression of dominance. She'd deliberately taunted him, admittedly inviting retaliation, and he'd chosen a very male way of showing her that he wouldn't allow her to get away with it.

Inwardly seething but not deigning to reply or even give in to the temptation to slap him, which would no doubt amuse him further, she turned and walked from him toward the house, but when she reached the steps he was right behind her.

Inside it was warm and seemed stuffy. Her father was seeing people off at the front door. As Alysia and Chase approached he said, ''There you are! Come and say good-night to Howard and Mollie, Alysia.''

She expected Chase to leave her. Instead he stayed at her side, and when the Franklins had left he said, ''I'll be off, too.''

''It's early!'' Spencer protested. ''The young ones

are still dancing—why don't you two go and join them? I think Alysia deserves to enjoy herself now."

"Alysia?" Chase turned to her, the perfect picture of courtesy.

"Thank you," she said precisely, "but I have a headache, and the music is a bit loud."

"Perhaps you'd rather go to bed," he suggested, his tone all concern, but his eyes held a wicked challenge.

She kept her own face schooled to a polite mask. "I'll see our guests off first," she told him. "You said you were going?"

Her father looked at her with surprise, but Chase gave her an appreciative grin and said, "If you're not going to partner me after all."

The grin was amazingly attractive. He seemed to have forgotten his flare of temper in the garden and the devastating way he'd expressed it. Now he regarded it as some kind of joke.

Alysia said, letting her eyes show her angry contempt, "I know you've enjoyed yourself."

"Even more than I anticipated," he assured her. "Thank you for making the evening so—stimulating."

Her eyelids flickered and she fought the impulse to look at her father to see if he was catching any hint of the undercurrents.

To her relief, Chase turned to him, shaking his hand. "A great party."

Spencer beamed. "Alysia did a wonderful job."

"Really, all I did was hire the caterers," she protested mildly. But pleasure at her father's rare praise warmed her cheeks and a spot somewhere in her midriff.

Verne Hastie came to say goodbye, and Alysia fixed a hostess smile on her face, turning from his beery breath as he kissed her cheek, his big hands squeezing her bare shoulders.

"We should entertain more often," Spencer suggested when he'd closed the door on the last of the guests. "The *Clarion's* a family paper—the staff needs to feel a part of it."

"Of the family?" Her father was proud of the Kingsley tradition, of his ancestry and of the *Clarion's* long—by New Zealand standards—history, but tonight was the first time she'd heard him claim the paper's staff as family.

"The younger ones," he said vaguely, "need to feel they belong. I lost two good people this year. Moving on."

But he was gaining another in the New Year— Alysia. Who wouldn't be leaving. She said, "Not many people nowadays stay with a company for life."

"Pity. No sense of continuity, of loyalty."

Chase ought to be held for a time by loyalty, by gratitude for the fast series of promotions he'd enjoyed under Spencer's patronage.

But didn't Spencer see that the very ambition he had admired and fostered in the younger man must inevitably lead to his desertion?

Alysia said, "Chase Osborne can't rise any higher at the *Clarion,* can he?" The Kingsleys always retained the top positions. It was one of the few truly family newspapers left.

Her father's gaze was penetrating while at the same time she had the impression his mind wasn't fully on their conversation. "I didn't train up a man like Chase to lose him to some big city corporation. He knows I'll see him right.''

Had Chase already been looking elsewhere? Alysia wondered later as she prepared for bed. Was that what was behind the promotion, the creation of a prestigious new position for him?

But in a year or two would that be enough to hold him, in a job where he could go no further?

She turned on her pillow and told herself it didn't matter if he left for better prospects, except that her father would be disappointed. And probably furious.

Chase Osborne was an opportunist by nature. Witness the way he'd climbed the ladder of success from lowly agricultural reporter to his present position, while older and more experienced staff remained stuck in the newsroom.

He was her father's blue-eyed boy—except that his eyes were actually an uncomfortably knowing hazel-green—and she gathered that his meteoric rise had created some antipathy among other employees. Chase apparently cared for the criticism no more than Spencer did. Those who were jealous or aggrieved either accepted the changes or left.

As she began to drift into sleep she found herself reliving the kiss under the pepper tree, vividly recalling every detail.

With an effort she opened her eyes, and restlessly turned on the pillow.

Chase Osborne believed in making the most of his chances. In the darkened garden he'd acted true to type—stung by her less than enthusiastic reaction to him and his promotion, and perhaps aided by a certain amount of alcohol which might have blunted some natural inhibition about kissing the boss's daughter.

He'd wanted to make her succumb, to assert the most primitive kind of male power because she'd shown him how little the other kind impressed her.

Maybe he was regretting it now. If she'd complained to her father he might have found himself less in favor. That would have been a setback to his flagrant ambition.

Contemplating the thought briefly, she quickly discarded it. Spencer would tell her she was making a mountain out of a molehill—if he believed her at all. Bitter memory rose to haunt her, and she determinedly pushed it away.

Put the kiss down to an excess of Christmas spirit and forget it.

Surprisingly difficult. She lay wakeful for ages, plagued by images of a dark head bowed over her, a glint of laughter in moonlit eyes, a warm masculine mouth confidently moving on hers, hard arms holding her firmly but not cruelly.

And she woke in the morning with the scent of the pepper tree still in her dream memory.

Chapter Two

The traffic light changed from red to green. Alysia turned the snappy little blue Toyota and it moved forward, then inexplicably stopped, stranding her in the middle of the intersection.

Other cars maneuvered around the stationary vehicle as she vainly pumped the accelerator and switched the key off and on.

Clenching both hands on the steering wheel, she gave vent to an expletive that would have shocked her father, before getting out and gratefully accepting the help of a couple of hefty male passersby who pushed the car to the side of the road.

"Want me to take a gander at the engine?" one asked.

"Thanks, but no." Amateur tinkering might void the guarantee.

The other Samaritan, a blond young man with a cocky air, offered hopefully, "I can give you a lift. My car's over there."

Alysia shook her head and brushed back a strand of hair escaping her ponytail. "I'll be fine," she said firmly. "My father's office is quite close. Thanks for your help."

He stood by as she took her purse and shopping bags from the car, locked the doors and walked away. When she glanced back he was still watching. Damn.

The late-afternoon sun beat hotly on her shoulders, bared by the tiny, sleeveless pink top she wore with a short denim skirt. Scientists had been warning of ozone depletion over New Zealand for years now. And summer was early this year. Christmas was still two weeks away.

At the *Clarion* Building she paused, and unconsciously took a slightly deeper breath before ascending the worn marble steps into the dim chill of the imposing old building. Next year she'd be doing this every day. Working in the newsroom with other reporters, she reminded herself. Not in the print room with its huge machines, echoing spaces and hidden corners.

She left her keys and purchases with the receptionist, then went up the brass-edged stairs and along a corridor to the office suite at the end.

A word processor hummed on the desk in the outer office, but there was no sign of Glenys Heath, her father's longtime secretary. The inner door was ajar. Tapping on the panels, Alysia pushed it wide and walked in.

Spencer was rummaging in a drawer behind the desk while Chase Osborne lounged against one side of it, his hands in his pockets. He looked up, giving her a faint, questioning smile, and straightened.

Spencer lifted his head, a sheet of paper in his

hand. "Here it is!" he said, handing the paper to
Chase before he noticed his daughter. "Alysia, my
dear! This is a surprise." He smiled at her, so evi-
dently happy to see her that she flushed with pleasure.

Chase said, "I'll leave you."

"No need," Spencer assured him. "Alysia won't
mind waiting while we go over the figures, will you,
Alysia? Get her a chair, Chase."

Alysia murmured that of course she didn't mind,
and sank into the chair that Chase unnecessarily
placed for her.

"I think I can follow these okay," he told Spencer,
glancing at the sheet of paper.

Holding out his hand for it, Spencer said a mite
testily, "We'll just check them together. Excuse us,
my dear."

Alysia slipped her leather bag from her shoulder,
folded her hands in her lap on top of it and placed
her ankles together while the two men murmured over
the document before them.

She deduced that Chase was perfectly able to understand without Spencer's help, and when she looked
up she found that instead of following the finger her
father was running down a column, he had lifted his
head slightly and was idly staring at her.

Alysia blinked, and he gave her an almost conspir-
atorial smile before his attention returned to the paper.

Alysia shifted her feet, crossing her ankles and
tucking them to one side. As if he'd caught the movement from the corner of his eye, Chase's attention
strayed again, and she was aware that he was inter-
estedly inspecting her ankles, then her calves right up
to where her skirt stopped above her knees.

Resisting the urge to tug at the skirt, she curled her

fingers around the bag in her lap. Chase's eyes swept up to her face, and he smiled openly before lowering his head and concentrating on what her father had to say.

He didn't look up again, and Alysia, after gazing at the art prints on the cream-painted walls, found herself studying the strong male hand that Chase had spread on the desk to brace himself as he bent over Spencer's shoulder. He had long fingers with short, almost square nails. His sleeves were rolled to the elbow, and his arm, sporting a businesslike stainless-steel watch, looked muscular and lightly tanned under a dusting of hair. She recalled how strongly it had held her three nights ago, how his fingers had combed through her hair and cradled her nape. Reluctant heat invaded her.

At last her father stopped talking, and Chase said patiently, "Okay, I've got that," before picking up the paper and folding it.

Spencer said, "What about a drink after work, Chase? Get Howard along. We need to do some preliminary planning of the home improvement supplement."

If Chase was put out at the demand on his supposedly free time, he didn't show it. "If you like," he said easily. About to leave, he paused as Alysia opened her mouth to speak, then changed her mind. His brows lifted in faint interrogation. "Something wrong?"

Alysia shook her head. To her father, she said, "My car broke down. I've called the garage to get the keys from reception and fetch it, and I was going to ask you for a lift. But if you're not coming straight home—"

Spencer frowned. "You haven't run out of petrol?"

Chase was trying not to grin, she thought. "I have plenty of petrol," she said, her chin lifting. "Teething troubles, I suppose." The car was brand-new.

Her father snorted. "I'll have something to say to the dealer about that." His face clearing somewhat, he suggested, "No reason why you shouldn't come with us. In fact we could all have dinner afterward. Save you fixing a meal."

"I can get a taxi." It was much too hot to walk.

Spencer overrode her, apparently unwilling to relinquish his solution. "Tell Howard he's invited to dinner, too," he ordered Chase. "He'll have to let his wife know."

Seated on a deep upholstered banquette flanking a low polished table, Alysia was next to Chase as they were served predinner drinks.

Howard produced a briefcase and opened a folder. "This is a preliminary draft of the home improvement supplement, but I think we can do better than last year, if we increase the ratio of straight advertisements—"

The three men bent over the folder, effectively blocking Alysia out. Spencer, with an air of giving her a treat, had ordered the cocktail of the day for her, and it had come in a wide, shallow glass decorated with a cherry and a tiny pink parasol. She sipped at it slowly until only a film of creamy foam remained, then sat idly opening and shutting the parasol.

"Alysia?" Chase's voice was in her ear, and she looked up to find his face quite close. The other two men were still engrossed in discussion. "Another drink?"

"No thanks." She shut the parasol decisively and placed it in her glass.

Chase's gaze followed the movement. "How was it?"

"The way it looked," she answered succinctly.

He gave a small, almost silent laugh. "Pink and sweet," he said, following her exactly. "Didn't you like it?"

"It was fine. I just don't need another."

He was still looking at her rather curiously, humor curling his mouth, when Spencer called his attention back to business.

After the waitress led them to their table it was Chase who pulled out a chair for Alysia between him and her father. The discussion continued throughout the meal.

"Our clients will provide most of the copy," Howard said.

Chase leaned back in his chair and picked up his wine glass. "Half the PR people who write those advertorials can't even spell, let alone string a literate sentence together."

"So we edit it!" Howard spread his hands. "That's what we pay sub-editors for."

"Advertorial?" Alysia queried.

Howard explained. "Articles about our advertisers' products."

"I know," she answered. "Disguised advertising. A cheap way to fill pages."

Chase gave her a considering look. "You have a problem with it?"

At journalism school this subject had been debated

quite hotly. "I think people should know when
they're reading puff for the paper's clients, not a real
product comparison. Will the supplement be labeled
as advertising?"

Spencer said impatiently, "People wouldn't read
it."

"They would if they're interested in the featured
products," she argued.

"You don't think," Chase asked her, "that our
readers are astute enough to know that a glowing ar-
ticle cheek by jowl with an ad for the product is a
promo?"

"A lot of people trust a newspaper to deliver im-
partial opinions."

"Certainly, in the news pages—"

Spencer interrupted brusquely. "People who don't
advertise with us can't expect free publicity, Alysia.
Just let us get on with our planning, my dear."

Alysia swallowed a protest. She might have paper
qualifications but that didn't give her any clout with
these experienced men. "Yes, of course," she said
quietly.

Chase's eyes were still on her, as if she'd intrigued
him, although her views couldn't be new to any sea-
soned newspaperman. "I'm interested in what Alysia
has to say."

"I've said it." She looked down at her plate and
speared a morsel of pineapple.

"We value your opinion, I'm sure." Her father
gave her a perfunctory smile, but she was more conscious of Chase's concentrated gaze. "Now, Chase,
if we have copy from advertisers there'll be no need
to send staffers…"

No use expecting her father to listen seriously to

her. Even though these days he bought her cocktails and took her along to an impromptu business dinner instead of treating her to ice-cream cones and G-rated films. Maybe parents never really accepted that their children had grown up.

When they'd had coffee Chase pushed his cup aside. "Thanks for the meal, Spencer. Shall we call it a night?"

Howard said, "I want to talk to Spencer about a problem with the classifieds."

Spencer called the waiter for more coffee, but Chase and Alysia both shook their heads.

"You don't need me anymore," Chase said. Again his eyes lighted on Alysia, with that new and disconcerting intentness. "Alysia looks tired. If you two want to stay on, I can take her home."

"I don't mind waiting," Alysia said.

But Spencer waved a hand benevolently and said, "Go with Chase, my dear. I'm sorry if this is a bit tedious for you."

Didn't he know she wanted to be involved in anything to do with the paper? It was her future. "It isn't at all—"

But Chase was already on his feet, and she had little choice. Gathering up her bag, she said goodnight to Howard and walked beside Chase to the entrance, then into the cooler night air in the car-park.

Chase paused outside the doorway and let out a brief, whistling breath.

"You didn't need to offer to take me home," Alysia said. "It's out of your way—"

"No problem." He curled his fingers around her arm in a light hold. "I'm grateful for the excuse."

Alysia was silent, and as they neared his car he said, "Sorry. That was tactless."

Not sure if the apology was for the implication that he'd wanted to get away from her father, or for suggesting that taking her home was no more than a pretext, she said coolly, "It's all right, Mr. Osborne."

He unlocked the passenger door and turned his head to glance at her probingly as he opened it.

With careful grace Alysia sank into the seat and waited while he closed the door.

When he slid in beside her he didn't immediately start the engine. Instead, his hands resting on the steering wheel, he turned to her and queried, "Mr. Osborne? We've known each other since you were a skinny little schoolgirl, Alysia."

Alysia had been nearly sixteen when Chase came to work for the *Clarion*. Leaving school eighteen months later, she had completed her Bachelor of Commerce in Auckland, several hours south of Waikura, before enrolling in journalism school still farther south in Wellington for a graduate diploma.

And in those few years Chase Osborne had climbed through several grades to chief reporter. And now deputy editor, although he couldn't be more than thirty.

"I might have been skinny then," Alysia said, "but actually I was tall for my age."

His mouth curved. "And you're not skinny any longer."

His eyes remained on her face, but she recalled his almost absentminded assessment of her legs when she'd sat in her father's office, and again the memory of that devastating kiss under the pepper tree surfaced, tingling in her blood.

"All grown up, in fact," Chase said. "But I hope you don't expect me to call you Miss Kingsley."

"I'm not a snob."

"No?"

Alysia stirred, and her bare arm brushed Chase's sleeve.

Turning away from him, she pulled her safety belt from its housing and clicked it into position.

She lifted an errant strand of hair from her cheek and put it behind her ear, then sat with her eyes focused straight ahead. The car park was lit with street lamps, and a few spiky cabbage trees shivered in a breeze, their slim, patterned trunks rising from floodlit flowerbeds.

Chase switched on the key and the engine murmured into life. He swung the car onto the road, drove through two sets of traffic lights and turned along the riverside. Between the boathouses and marine businesses, glimpses of dark water reflected wavery ribbons of light.

"So you have your own car now?" Chase asked.

Not sure why she felt defensive, Alysia said, "My father bought it as a graduation present."

"Congratulations on your diploma, by the way."

"Thank you."

"I was surprised you decided to do a journalism course after all."

"Why?" Surely nothing could have been more obvious.

"I had the idea you didn't particularly care for the newspaper business. We don't see you down at the office much."

Alysia felt her skin tighten but she kept her voice

calm. "The last few years I've been studying," she reminded him. "Of course I care—I'm a Kingsley."

"Ah...the Kingsley dynasty," he murmured.

"I prefer to call it a tradition." Alysia didn't like the irony coloring his voice.

He was silent for a couple of seconds. "Spencer doesn't have a lot of time for high-powered career women."

Spencer tended toward archaic views on women in business—in fact on women in general—but he didn't have a choice in her case. The newspaper was a family institution, and Alysia was the only family he had. When she told him she wanted to first gain a commerce degree and then study journalism for a year, he had talked approvingly about the value of qualifications.

"I'm starting at the *Clarion* after the New Year," she said. "Hasn't my father mentioned it?"

"He suggested we make a place for you."

Alysia guessed from the reserve in his voice that Chase Osborne didn't approve of nepotism. Too bad. It might be old-fashioned, but it was the way the *Clarion* had always operated, each generation succeeding the last. One day the newspaper would pass to her. Her father couldn't deny her that.

Her hands clasped almost painfully together. "I'm qualified."

She willed away a nasty, sick feeling in her stomach. She was an adult now. Time she acted like one, instead of like some scared little schoolgirl.

Chase made a sound like a short, scornful little laugh. "You have a brand-new diploma."

"Even you must have been a beginner once." She knew she sounded snippy. "I don't mind starting at the bottom. Like my father.'' Though heir to the business, he'd begun as a junior reporter, straight from school.

"He's a good journo," Chase conceded. "I've learned a lot from him."

"And so will I be," Alysia asserted.

"You mean it's in the blood?"

The mockery in the remark stung, although he couldn't know how it reached a particularly sensitive place in her heart. Her throat tightened. "Anyone can learn."

They reached the house and she was out of the car before Chase came round it to open the door for her.

"I'll see you inside." He followed her up the wide path to the front door and waited while she opened her bag, fumbling for her keys. She let out a short, annoyed exclamation and he said, "What's wrong?"

"I assumed I'd be coming home with Dad. I've left my house key on the ring with the car keys."

"So you can't get in."

"Damn! How stupid!" She glared at the firmly locked front door as if that might miraculously open it.

"No hidden keys?"

"We don't do that."

"Probably wise. What about open windows?"

"The bathroom, maybe. But it's too high."

"Show me."

"You can't…" But she showed him all the same, and then watched as he swung onto the roof of the veranda.

He moved with grace and economy and Alysia was unwillingly fascinated by the play of muscles under his shirt, the lithe masculinity of his body. Sternly she thrust away the stirring of sexual curiosity.

Chase made surefootedly for the slightly open window, thrust it wide and hoisted himself through the narrow space.

A few minutes later lights went on and he opened the door for her, stepping back to allow her in. He was fishing in his pocket with his left hand, holding his right hand up while blood trickled from the knuckles.

"What have you done?"

"Grazed myself getting the window open properly. There wasn't much room. It's nothing." He'd found a handkerchief and was clumsily trying to wrap it about his bleeding hand. "I don't think I've messed the carpet. Can you tie this for me?"

"Come upstairs again and I'll get a plaster for it. Come on," Alysia insisted as he looked about to argue.

She led him to the main bathroom, placed her bag on the floor and took a first-aid box from the cupboard under the hand basin. She unscrewed the cap on a bottle of disinfectant. "Is it dirty?"

"No. Just pour a bit of that on," he said, holding his hand over the basin. "It'll kill any lurking germs."

He winced slightly as she did so, and she murmured, "Maybe we should have diluted this. It stings."

"I noticed." He seemed very close, watching her as she swabbed the wound dry with a piece of gauze and pressed a plaster over it. Although he shifted back a little while she replaced the disinfectant and plasters, she was conscious of him right behind her.

When she turned he didn't move, and she found herself trapped against the basin. She raised wary eyes, and caught a strange look in his. A look that seemed attentive and faintly puzzled. Without speaking he lowered his head, pressing a quick, warm kiss on her mouth.

It was over before she had a chance to either reciprocate or protest, or even decide which she wanted to do.

"Thank you," he said. And still he didn't move away, his steady gaze questioning.

She stared back, refusing to evade the challenge.

He was too adept at finding vulnerable areas of her psyche. A reporter's instinct, she guessed, that told him where to dig for what lay under the surface. For what people preferred to keep hidden.

He knew that since the kiss in the garden she'd been unwillingly attracted to him. No doubt the knowledge gave him great satisfaction. But that didn't mean she'd give in to the attraction.

His smile widened a little, and then his head dipped again.

Alysia whipped her own head back, her hands clutching at the cold porcelain of the basin behind her.

Chase straightened. Alysia tried to keep her eyes steady and indifferent. She still felt a tingle of surprised pleasure on her lips. But mingled with the pleasure was hostility, resentment that *this* man could produce that sensation.

At last Chase took a step away, then another. Blocking the doorway, he cast a lightning glance over her, and she realized that she was taut as a bowstring, her body curved so that her breasts and hips were thrust forward. Hastily she readjusted her stance, releasing her grip on the basin to bring her arms protectively across her midriff.

Chase laughed then, his eyes going glittery. She must have imagined that fleeting tenderness, there was no sign of it now. The thought pierced her, unexpectedly poignant.

"That cocktail," he said conversationally, "was it chilled?"

Alysia blinked at the non sequitur. "Yes. There was ice in it."

"I thought so." He stood there a moment longer, surveying her in a not unfriendly way but with a hint of sarcasm in his slight smile. Then he sketched her a salute. "Tell your father he ought to get a burglar-proof catch on that window. Good night—I'll find my own way out."

She heard his quick footsteps on the stairs, and the forceful closing of the front door, and then the distinct sound of whistling as he went on down the path.

Pink and sweet—and cold. That's what he thought of her, Alysia acknowledged irritably. Translated it meant insipid and uninteresting.

It didn't matter. What Chase Osborne thought of her was a matter of total indifference to her. Wasn't it?

Chapter Three

Alysia and her father spent Christmas Day with his sister in Auckland. Aunt Patricia's children were all married but some of them brought along their families for Christmas dinner.

Perhaps because she'd been an only child herself, Alysia enjoyed the children, willingly keeping them amused while their parents relaxed after a too-large midday meal.

At the end of the day she helped her cousin Valda pack children and their paraphernalia into the family station wagon.

Stuffing a teddy bear into a carry bag, Valda asked her curiously, "Do you really want to work at the *Clarion?*"

Alysia straightened from fastening a child's safety belt. "Of course."

Valda cast her a shrewd look. "To please your father?"

Alysia tucked an errant strand of her hair into its clasp. "To carry on the family tradition."

"Robbie!" Momentarily distracted, Valda admonished her younger son. "Leave your sister alone!" Turning back to Alysia, she looked at her speculatively. "I wondered if you chose to study journalism in Wellington just for a chance to spread your wings. Between your father and my mother you'd led a pretty sheltered life."

While Alysia was at university she had boarded with her aunt and uncle. Her father had vetoed her sharing accommodation with friends, seemingly convinced that student houses were both expensive and dens of iniquity. And Aunt Patricia had discharged her responsibility very conscientiously.

"I had a good time while I was at university," Alysia said. "Your mother never locked me in."

Valda laughed. "Good for you. Well, if you're happy—*Robbie*, I said *stop that!* Where's that husband of mine?"

"I'll find him," Alysia offered, and made for the house.

Between Christmas and New Year, Alysia drove to Auckland to help her university friends celebrate one of their birthdays.

Seated round a large table in an upmarket restaurant, the group bantered with the waitress, laughed at corny jokes and enjoyed being together again.

They had reached the dessert course when Alysia saw Chase Osborne across the room, dining tête-à-tête with a dark, sultry young woman wearing a slinky black dress that showed off her generously curved figure.

The woman was talking, using her hands for emphasis, showing off long, elegant nails painted a brilliant pink, and occasionally pushing at the riot of loose curls about her face. Chase smiled now and then at something she said, and once laughed outright.

That was when he noticed Alysia, his eyes catching hers across the room, laughter still on his mouth as he lifted a hand to her.

She felt the impact of that look like a small shock, and nodded to him, mustering a smile.

His eyes took in her companions and then returned to his partner. Alysia tore her gaze away. The birthday boy had called for another bottle of wine and was refilling glasses over laughing protests.

When the waiter carried in a cake ablaze with candles the party became even more lively, attracting the notice of other diners, some of whom good-naturedly joined in the singing of "Happy Birthday." Determined not to glance in Chase's direction again, Alysia was nevertheless acutely aware that he too had looked up at the cheers and laughter.

As the group left the restaurant, the host's unsteady steps being hilariously directed by two other young men, Chase and his companion were in the foyer. With a word to the woman, he crossed to Alysia and drew her aside. "You're not driving home tonight?"

"I'm staying with my cousin in Auckland."

"Did you bring your own car to the restaurant?"

"No. What does it have to do with—"

"I can give you a lift."

Astonished, she looked past him to where the sultry beauty waited. "Your girlfriend might object to that."

"Your father might object to you being driven by some young idiot who's over the limit."

"My friends are not idiots. Donna doesn't drink at all, and she'll be driving some of us home. The others are taking a taxi. Not that it need concern you."

He released her arm without apology. "I'm glad to hear it. You'll be all right, then?"

"I'm not a silly teenager, Chase."

"Okay. You go home tomorrow?"

"Yes."

"Me, too." He cast a comprehensively critical glance over her friends in the background. "See you back in Waikura, then." He walked off to rejoin his dinner date, who tucked a hand into his arm and lifted her face to give him a dazzling smile.

Alysia left the restaurant with the others and tried to share in their hilarity as they made for the car and piled in to it. She had enjoyed the chance to relax, be young and a little goofy with her friends. But now they seemed very juvenile, and their tipsy humor failed to amuse her anymore. Somehow tonight was spoiled for her.

"Your boss's daughter?" Mariette asked Chase as they walked to his car.

"Yes." He'd told her that when he went to speak with Alysia. To make sure she wasn't going to do anything silly and dangerous.

"Is she underage?"

"For drinking? No." Feeling a need to justify himself, Chase added, "But her father's very protective."

Mariette gave him a sideways look. "Seems he's not the only one. She didn't look too thrilled with you."

"She doesn't like me much," Chase admitted shortly, not sure why that irritated him.

Before the Christmas party he'd scarcely thought of Alysia Kingsley at all. She'd only appeared during vacations from school or university, not changing a great deal from the quiet, pretty, but rather colorless kid he'd first met.

At the party he'd noted that the duckling who had never been ugly was definitely a swan, but it wasn't until he'd found her in the garden, looking pensive and somehow poignant, that he'd had to quell a surprising impulse to take her in his arms, not only to comfort, but to find out what that slight but feminine body would feel like snuggled against his.

Her instant resentment of his presence, the fierceness of her unsuspected dislike, had if anything heightened the sexual curiosity she'd aroused. He'd been unable to resist kissing her even though he knew she wouldn't welcome it. Not at all his usual style.

And despite her effort to freeze him off he'd recognized the subtle signs of her instinctive response.

She was a bundle of contradictions. A spoiled daddy's girl who somehow managed to seem insecure, vulnerable. Docile and compliant with her father, but capable of a cutting arrogance with lesser mortals. She didn't hide her hostility to Chase, yet he'd swear she felt the same sexual buzz he did when he touched her.

And tonight he shouldn't even be thinking about Alysia Kingsley while another woman hung on his arm saying something he hadn't even heard. He smiled down at Mariette. "Sorry, what did you say?"

"Are we going back to my place?"

Although he'd had every intention of doing so when he phoned and suggested a date, Chase shook his head. "I'll drop you off," he said, pleading pressure of work. It wouldn't be fair to accept the invitation when another woman was annoyingly uppermost in his thoughts. He'd drive to Waikura tonight.

"Good birthday party?" Spencer enquired at breakfast on Monday. Alysia hadn't returned from Auckland until late on Sunday night, and when she'd let herself in the house had been in darkness.

"Fine," she answered automatically. "It was nice seeing my friends again."

"You have friends in Waikura," Spencer commented.

"Not really, now." Away at boarding school through her high school years, she had lost touch with her earlier playmates.

In the days that followed, making the most of her last long holiday, Alysia swam, pottered around the house and indulged herself with books that weren't prescribed for exams.

On New Year's Eve, dressed in a brief tube top and shorts, she was lying on a rug under the pepper tree, absorbed in a fat romantic historical saga, when Chase found her.

He'd knocked at the front door and, getting no reply, walked around the back. Realizing that Alysia was unaware of his presence, he'd spent a few minutes contemplating the picture she made, without the prickly defenses she always assumed in his presence. Lying on her side, her head propped on one hand, her knees drawn up, she might have been still a teenager, but for the decidedly womanly curve of her hip, and the glimpse of a cleavage afforded by the skimpy top she wore.

Her expression was absorbed, the jade-green eyes

half hidden by long lashes, her lips innocent of makeup and slightly parted. He watched her tongue briefly touch the upper one as she turned a page, and his body tightened and stirred.

He remembered the taste of her mouth, remembered how despite her maddening refusal to allow her rigidly held body to accept his embrace, that mouth, which had mocked and defied and flicked him on the raw, felt soft and sweet and incredibly seductive. A contradiction.

Looking at her body now, Chase's mouth curved in self-mockery. He could have sworn that when he first kissed her she'd almost opened up to him, at least physically, and then she'd stalked off without a word. Banged down the shutters in his face. And, but for an occasional brief, unwitting chink, she'd kept them down ever since.

If she thought he'd back off she could think again. She'd thrown out a challenge and he'd never refused one in his life. One day he'd make her acknowledge that this unsettling desire to touch, to explore, to *know,* wasn't all on his side.

She might the boss's daughter, heiress to Kingsley's little kingdom, but she'd learn that sex was the great leveler. When it came down to it, a naked princess was like any other woman without her clothes.

Alysia turned another page. A shadow fell across it and Chase's deep voice said, "Hi, there."

"Chase!" At first she couldn't see him properly against the sun as she scrambled to her feet. "What are you doing here?"

His eyes seemed focused on her legs, and he took his damned time about getting them back to her face, lingering along the way on her bare midriff and the strip of thin knit fabric that clung to her breasts.

"What do you want?" she asked him, disconcerted by the unabashed stare, although it seemed almost impersonal, his eyes veiled.

Chase raised his black brows slightly. "A cat may look..." he murmured.

"What?"

He laughed softly in his throat, and to her annoyance she felt a warm shiver curl her toes and feather up her spine. "Nothing," he said. "Your father wants a folder that he left in his study." His eyes drifted to the book that lay face down on the blanket.

Flustered, and convinced he despised her taste in literature, Alysia started toward the house, tossing breeze-blown hair away from her eyes. "I thought you were the deputy editor, not the errand boy."

"I had to pass by here on my way to see someone, and Spencer asked me to call in and fetch the folder for him."

"I could have brought it down if he'd phoned."

"I guess he thought you'd be...busy."

He'd just seen how "busy" she was. She opened the back door. Her eyes took a little while to adjust as she led him through the big kitchen and along the wide, dim passageway. Pushing open the door of her father's study, she paused to orient herself, and Chase stopped behind her—so close that she felt the brush of his clothes against her bare back.

Hastily she stepped into the room. "What folder is it that my father wants?"

"Gray. He said it should be on his desk." Chase walked past her. "That looks like it." He picked up a folder lying beside the computer on the big oak desk and flipped it open.

"Did he tell you to look inside it?" Alysia asked sharply.

Chase glanced up, his eyes dark green and glinting. "He told me to check that the document he wanted is here."

"I see." What was it about this man that made her feel like an animal with its fur rubbed the wrong way? And react by hissing and clawing? "Is it?"

Chase looked down again, shuffled some papers and closed the folder. "Looks like it."

He seemed in no hurry, his attention taken by a silver-framed photograph on one corner of the desk, although he must have seen it before.

It was a picture of Alysia and her mother, taken at a fancy dress ball when Alysia was five years old. Chase's gaze slid from the photograph to her. "You have the same coloring," he said, "but you're not really much like your mother, are you?"

"No." She felt her shoulders go rigid and she waited for him to comment further.

"Whose idea was the outfit?"

She'd been dressed in a white tulle gown and a tall, pointed gold hat with a veil over long curls. As a child she'd been a true golden blonde; her hair had darkened to a more nondescript shade as she grew older. "Hers," she said. Her mother had made the costume, while Alysia watched excitedly and tried not to wriggle when the dress was pinned on for fittings.

Chase nodded, and strolled past her with the folder in his hand.

She was following when he reached the doorway

and turned abruptly so that she had to stop, too close to him for comfort. "Suits you," he said laconically.

"What?"

His gaze went over her shoulder to the photograph on the desk, then returned to her face, and he grinned outright. "See you, Alysia. I'll find my way out."

Alysia tore her indignant gaze from his back and swung to face the room. Her mother's face smiled obliquely at her, and she felt a familiar ache deep inside. On the evening of the fancy dress ball she'd truly felt like the fairy-tale princess she was supposed to be. Her father had seemed proud of her, and of her mother. His wife must have been pregnant then with the little boy who had later been stillborn.

Alysia had only dimly understood her parents' grief, but afterward she had always known that for Spencer she was second best. He was good to her— anyone would say he was a generous and even indulgent father—but sometimes she wished she'd been the boy he had really wanted.

Later in the evening she was sitting in the lounge with Spencer, watching a TV host trying to whip up a party atmosphere in the studio, when the phone rang.

Alysia went into the hallway to answer it.

"Alysia?" Chase sounded surprised. "I thought you'd be out partying tonight."

"Are *you?*" she countered.

He laughed. "I had some stuff to catch up on in the office, and I need to ask your father something. But I may go down to the Old Quay later and see the New Year in. What about you?"

The town's young people traditionally gathered by

the river to celebrate the passing of each year. "That isn't an invitation, is it?" Alysia asked lightly. And then bit her lip because perhaps she'd sounded as though she were angling for one.

He said, without missing a beat, "Certainly, if you like."

Alysia forced a laugh. "Don't worry, I won't take you up on it."

"Why not?"

"You didn't mean it."

"I don't say things I don't mean, Alysia."

"Thank you for asking me," she said formally, "but really—"

Her father came out of the lounge, his brows raised interrogatively, and she said hurriedly, "It's Chase," and handed him the phone.

He took it from her. "Chase?"

Alysia went back to the TV program, shutting the door on the conversation.

When Spencer returned he gave her a penetrating look. "Chase said he'll pick you up at eleven."

She looked up in dismay. "But I didn't say I'd go—"

"Why not?" Spencer inquired brusquely. "Girl of your age shouldn't be sitting at home with her father on New Year's Eve."

"I don't mind! I'll phone Chase back and tell him I'm not coming…"

Spencer frowned. "He knows you don't have any other plans—I told him. You can do with some young company."

"I'm not desperate!" She could have gone to Auckland and partied with her friends, only she hadn't fancied driving so far on her own in the holiday traffic. "He doesn't need to take pity on me."

Spencer gave a short bark of a laugh. "Nonsense. You're an attractive girl, Alysia. And I won't let you snub the boy. Of course you'll go with him."

As if Chase would care. He'd have laughed off her refusal and found someone else to accompany him.

But her father's face as he picked up the newspaper he'd already read and shook it open told her he wasn't going to listen to argument.

A familiar deep-down loneliness gripped her. Of course her father was fond of her but his parenting style was heavy-handed. He gave praise when he saw it was merited, physical affection rarely and clumsily, and when he laid down the law he expected no argument. In many ways he scarcely knew her at all. After her mother died they'd been apart more than together.

They had lost each other, Alysia thought sadly. The conduit for their relationship had been the woman they both loved. Since her death they'd been blindly fumbling in the darkness, occasionally blundering together for a brief moment of understanding, of sharing, but without the blessing of continued safe, secure contact.

"I'll go and get changed," she said, resigned, and Spencer looked up, his expression relenting into an approving smile.

Chapter Four

Alysia met Chase at the door, wearing white jeans and a loose, light sweater with a wide neck.

He was in jeans too, and a casual shirt. He smiled at her, but his eyes turned wary as they met the rebellious sparkle in hers. "Ready?"

"Yes." She called good-night to her father, then came outside, evading the hand Chase offered as she came down the steps, and let him open the door of his car for her.

He slipped in beside her. "You look great."

"Thank you." She was gazing out the windshield, embarrassed that her father had manipulated Chase into this with heavy hints about her barren social life.

Chase hesitated, then started the engine. The car glided away from the house.

"I thought you'd be in Auckland tonight," she said.

"Why?"

"Isn't your girlfriend there?"

"Girlfriend?"

"The one I saw you with in Auckland?"

"Ah…Mariette."

"That's a pretty name."

"She's a pretty girl," Chase said blandly. "But I don't know her well enough to call her my girlfriend."

"Yet?" she asked pointedly.

He shrugged, then turned to her. "You're not jealous, are you?"

Alysia cast him a withering look, and he laughed.

In the distance lights winked, and as they neared the river they could see the Old Quay, colored bulbs strung about its edge, floodlights trained on the crowd gyrating to live music.

"Looks like it's jumping." Chase slowed, looking for a place to park. Miraculously he found a space and slid the car expertly into it. Instead of getting out, he turned to Alysia and said, "What's the matter?"

"Nothing." She fumbled for the door handle but he put out a hand and caught hers in his warm fingers, stopping her. The movement brought him closer, and she breathed in his clean, warm, male scent.

"Are you missing your friends?"

Her head turned sharply. "You don't need to patronize the poor little rich girl—"

Chase's brows lifted. "Is that how you see yourself?"

"*No!*" What a revolting thought. "Of course not."

He looked as if he doubted it, his eyes suddenly searching. "You lost your mother when you were very young."

"Thirteen. My father's very good to me. And I

have plenty of friends. They just don't happen to live here."

She stirred under the steady gaze, pulled her hand away from his slackened hold and demanded rather imperiously, "Are we going to this party?"

"Sure." Without haste he got out, and by the time he'd come around the car she was already standing beside it.

The old grayed boards of the sturdily built quay, where in former days ships had tied up to load timber for markets in Australia and America, resounded to the thumping feet of dozens of dancing, swaying couples.

A waterside café in the old shipping building with its nineteenth-century clock tower spilled light from wide-open doors on people sitting around tables.

Occupants of fishing boats and pleasure crafts anchored nearby lounged on deck or perched atop cabin housing, watching the fun on shore.

Alysia and Chase reached the outskirts of the crowd on the wharf, and against the noise of the music he leaned down and said in her ear, "Dance?"

Alysia shrugged, took a couple of steps and turned to face him.

He smiled at her, and they tacitly moved into the rhythm of the music, two feet apart. Alysia shook back her hair, her eyes going dreamy, lids half closed as she moved her shoulders and hips and feet to the beat. Dancing relaxed her, made her feel free and happy.

Chase watched her, his own body lithely following the music, now and then an expression of something like curiosity lighting his eyes.

When the band stopped for a breather, and everyone clapped and stamped and whistled, he put a hand on Alysia's waist. "Would you like a drink?"

"I'd love one."

She smiled at him, for once letting down her guard, and he looked back at her, then smiled, too, looking suddenly younger and more approachable. "Let's see if we can fight our way to the bar."

He left her at the door of the crowded café and joined the throng about the counter, eventually returning bearing beer for himself and gin and bitters for her. "We'll be lucky to find a seat."

"Doesn't matter." She sipped at the cool drink.

"Let's move from here anyway." He urged her away from the crowd pressing into the café. A brown-eyed, olive-skinned girl waved to Alysia from a chair at one of the outdoor tables.

"Sandra!" Alysia went toward her, and Chase followed. "Sandra Ropata!" They had been good friends before Alysia went to boarding school. "I thought you'd left Waikura."

"Yeah, I went away to nursing school, and then I worked for a while in Auckland until a job came up at the local hospital. My parents always wanted me back here. You know my mum."

Alysia smiled. Sandra's mother headed a large, close-knit Maori family. Her greatest joy was to have all her brood around her, and there had always been a welcome for an extra cousin or two or stray visitors like Alysia.

A young man seated beside Sandra stood up. "Hey, come and sit down." By some sleight of hand he appropriated two empty chairs from adjoining tables to add to the four already occupied. "I'm Hurley," he said, and introductions were made all round.

When the music started again conversation was difficult, but during another lull, Hurley leaned across the table to speak to Chase. "You remind me of a kid I went to school with, way back. Can't remember his first name, but his last name was Jesson. We called him Jessie. Might be a cuzzie?"

"Charles Jesson. No, not a cousin."

Hurley snapped his fingers. "I remember now, we used to call him Charlie at first and he hated it, so then we made it Jessie and he hated that even more. Kids can be nasty little bastards."

"Yes," Chase said.

"Mind, he gave as good as he got. Had a temper, and he'd take anybody on, even blokes bigger than him."

"I guess I was oversensitive."

Hurley's jaw dropped, but he quickly recovered. "You?" he asked disbelievingly, and slapped the table, grinning. "You're having me on!"

Chase shook his head. "I gave up on Charles. When we moved again I told my new schoolmates my name was Chase. They had a bit of fun with that too, but I thought it sounded racier than Charles."

"Didn't you say your last name's Osborne?"

"My mother married a guy called Osborne." Chase looked coolly at the other man. "I took his name."

"Your mother—" Hurley met Chase's eyes and hastily swallowed whatever he'd been going to say. "So, what are you doing now, er, Chase?"

"Working for the *Clarion.*"

"Oh, I know!" Sandra interrupted. "You're the new deputy editor. There was a photo in the paper."

Hurley looked impressed. "Good on you! You

were always saying *I'll show you* when you were a kid.'' His eyes slid to Alysia and he grinned, looking back at Chase. ''Looks like you're doing very nicely, I reckon!''

''I am,'' Chase agreed calmly.

''Great! Course, you wouldn't have had such a hard time of it at school if we hadn't all been jealous.''

''Jealous?''

''Yeah, you know—always top of the class, and played hard and fast sport, too. You took everything so *seriously,* even football. As if it was life and death.'' Hurley grinned round at his table companions. ''The rest of us were stuffing around having a good time and there was old Jessie—sorry, Chase— showing us all up for the lazy slobs we were.'' He looked back at Chase. ''That's why half the class hated you. And the rest of us—we took our cue from the bullies,'' he admitted.

Chase was staring at him as if he couldn't believe what he was hearing. ''Jealous,'' he repeated, and shook his head. The music started again and he pulled Alysia to her feet. ''Dance with me,'' he said in her ear, against the volume of the speakers.

This time he wrapped her close to him, his arms around her. Fantastically, she had a fleeting impression that he needed some kind of comfort. She said, ''Where did you go to school?''

''What?'' He inclined his head closer.

Alysia went on tiptoe, her breath brushing his cheek. ''Where did you go to school with Hurley?''

''Here,'' he said, his cheek against hers. ''Not in your part of town. But right here in Waikura.''

Alysia missed a step, pulling back to look at him.

"Waikura?" She knew he couldn't hear her for the music, but her amazed face and the shaping of the word on her lips must have told him.

He grinned almost defiantly and bent down to enunciate every word very clearly. "Right…here…in Waikura," he repeated.

The others were dancing too, and their table was appropriated in their absence, but the men found enough room for the women to sit on the wide edging of the wharf. Alysia and Sandra had a lot to talk about, and Chase seemed at ease with the other men.

Later they danced again, and a minute before midnight a drumroll turned everyone's attention to the clock tower and the crowd began counting down the seconds.

As the clock hit midnight cheers and whistles and hooting erupted, and couples became locked in passionate embraces. Nearby, Sandra had her arms about Hurley's neck and was kissing him with abandon.

Chase, his arm on Alysia's waist, looked down at her with a half smile, his eyebrows lifted.

At least this time he was waiting for permission.

She'd had a good time and enjoyed dancing with him. The year was new, and she and Chase were shortly going to be working in the same office. Time to bury the hatchet, maybe.

On a surge of reckless anticipation, she lifted her face to him.

A flicker of expression that she couldn't read crossed his face, perhaps surprise. Then he bent and fitted his lips over hers.

His mouth was warm and exciting and inviting, and his hand pressed her a little closer to him, but he didn't pull her fully into his arms. Instead his fingers slipped around her nape, and her lips parted slightly, but he didn't take advantage of the tacit invitation. She felt he was holding back.

Someone started "Auld Lang Syne" and others joined in. When Chase drew away Alysia kept her eyes shut for a moment, and slowly opened them to see him looking almost as bemused as she felt, as if something unexpected had hit him. As if for once he wasn't quite sure of himself.

She swallowed, and then Sandra grabbed her hand and they were both swung into the circle of singers, with Chase holding her other hand.

Afterward he still held it as they walked back to his car.

Alysia was caught in a magic bubble that a wrong gesture or word could shatter. She didn't dare speak, hardly looking at him, but she was acutely conscious of his fingers curled about hers in a firm grip. When he released her to let her into the car she climbed in and clasped both hands in her lap.

On the way home she said, "Do many people know you grew up here?"

"It's no secret. But most people don't recognize me."

"What about my father?"

"He never asked."

"How old were you when your mother remarried?"

"I was eleven when she married my stepfather." He seemed to hesitate. "She wasn't married before."

Not married? "Then you were…"

"A bastard," Chase said laconically.

"I wasn't going to say that! I *wouldn't!*"

''There were plenty of kids and a few adults who didn't worry about saying it when I was growing up.''

Distressed for the child he had been, she said, ''That's awful!''

He shrugged. ''It was a long time ago. People are more broad-minded now.''

''Did you like your stepfather?''

''He was all right. He gave me his name, which was more than my real father had ever done for me.''

''He adopted you?''

''No. They changed my name by deed poll, but he never tried to be a father to me, something I thank him for.''

''Was your mother happy?''

''My mother was grateful.''

''I'm glad.'' It sounded a bit bleak, though. ''Who was your father?''

''I don't think even my mother knows that.''

She stared at him, remembering how Hurley had started to mention Chase's mother, and abruptly cut himself off.

His eyes fixed on the winding uphill road, he said remotely, ''The possible candidates are many. And none of them would have wanted to know. There are people in this town who'll remember my mother's... profession, like Hurley. You may as well hear it from me.''

Alysia felt a vicarious pain, imagining growing up with that background in a place like this. She wanted to comfort the boy he'd once been, but the man he had become wore a hardened expression that tacitly held her off. ''I'm so sorry, Chase.''

''I've got over it. And that's enough about my traumatic childhood.''

He had certainly risen above an appallingly unpromising start in life. But she wondered if anyone truly got over something like that.

They didn't speak again until he drew up outside her door, where the porch light glowed. She knew her father would have gone to bed.

"I really enjoyed that," she confessed.

"You hadn't expected to, had you?"

"Had you?"

"That's an odd question." He gave her a quizzical look, and then laughed softly. "I had a good time, too, Princess."

She opened her door and had got out by the time he had opened his. "I have my key this time," she assured him and went lightly up the steps.

Chase waited until she'd let herself in, then lifted a hand in farewell and got back in the car.

Could she be as artless and inexperienced as that kiss had suggested?

While they danced she seemed to have forgotten her customary defenses. When at midnight she'd looked up at him so expectantly, almost trustingly, he'd seen for a moment the girl-child he'd first met, making him hesitate.

He'd felt an obscure need to exercise restraint, and yet the chaste and nearly sexless kiss had tested his control. He'd wanted to gather her close, with a mixture of passion and protectiveness. Not the way he'd ever expected to feel about a woman with all the advantages enjoyed by Alysia Kingsley.

The summer days lazed on; cicadas shrilled throbbingly in every tree so that the air itself seemed to vibrate with their song. Bougainvillaea hung heavy on the fences, abundant swathes of purple and red. Alysia relied on several dips a day to keep her cool. She was emerging from the pool late one afternoon when her father appeared, accompanied by Chase.

"This is where you are!" Spencer exclaimed, and Chase strolled forward, forestalling her movement toward the towel draped over a green canvas lounger.

He took his time about handing it to her, unabashedly appreciating her figure in the clinging, wet swimsuit and letting his gaze drift down her legs.

Alysia held out her hand and he smiled at her as he gave her the towel. It was unfair, that smile. Far too sexy, and the way it lit his eyes removed the hint of harshness from his face.

"Thank you." She hoped he didn't notice the slight breathlessness in her voice before she wrapped the big towel about her, sarong-fashion.

"Chase is going to eat with us," her father informed her. "We have some business to discuss."

Chase said, "If that's all right with you."

"It's no problem."

Spencer's part-time housekeeper, a widow with dependent children, habitually froze a week's meals for him to heat in the microwave oven. Before the Christmas break she always stocked the freezer with dishes for two and took six weeks holiday with her family.

In the past Alysia had simply done a little housework and kept the place tidy but, free of holiday assignments for the first time in years, she'd found a pile of cookbooks on a shelf in the pantry, and begun experimenting.

"You're becoming quite a good cook," Spencer had told her approvingly, and she glowed.

* * *

She put on a cotton frock and sandals, rubbed her hair with a towel and briefly used a hand-dryer before combing it.

Smoothing on eyeshadow and lipstick, she noticed a faint color in her cheeks. Her eyes looked darker than usual, the pupils enlarged. Coming into the house after the blazing sun outside would have done that. And the heat was enough to make anyone a bit flushed.

As usual when Spencer had a business guest she said very little at the table.

Stacking the sweet dishes together at the end of the meal, she said, "I think I'll skip coffee, it's too hot for this weather. Shall I bring yours and Chase's to your study?"

Her father opted for the cooler terrace, and she promised, "I'll bring it out."

But as Spencer made for the terrace, Chase lingered, his hand on a chair back. "Need any help?" His glance took in the things remaining on the table.

Alysia shook her head. "I just stack them in the dishwasher."

Spencer had turned in the doorway, and she added hurriedly, "I won't be long."

When Alysia took them coffee the men were deep in discussion. Her father thanked her dismissively, and she reluctantly returned to the kitchen to finish clearing up.

The men's voices impinged on her awareness as she worked, but then there was a short silence followed by Chase's voice, sharp and urgent, calling her name.

Running to see what was the matter, she saw her father slumped in his chair, his face a strange grayish color and shiny with sweat, his breathing labored. Chase bent over him, a hand on his shoulder.

As Alysia appeared in the doorway Chase eased the older man off the chair and laid him on the hard tiles of the terrace. Scarcely looking up, he said, "Call an ambulance. I think he's having a heart attack."

Chapter Five

Hours later Alysia surfaced from her shock and terror.

Chase hadn't left her side from the time the ambulance team had arrived.

Now Spencer was in intensive care, his life dependent on tubes and monitors. "He's doing quite nicely," she'd been told. "Why don't you go home, try to sleep? We'll call you if there's any change."

In the anteroom she turned to Chase. "Any change? Does that mean if they think he's going to die?" She felt like a little girl again, begging for reassurance.

"It means if things change," Chase said firmly. "If he's well enough to talk to you...or if his condition deteriorates. They can't make promises."

His blunt honesty steadied her more than any false optimism would have done. "Thank you for coming with me."

"You'd better do as they suggest. He might need

you tomorrow—'' glancing at his watch, Chase amended that to ''—today, and you don't want to be half asleep with fatigue and worry. Why don't I take you home?''

Back at the house he switched on the hall light before she could do it herself. Looking down at her with compassion in his eyes, he said, ''You'd better get into bed.''

''Thank you...for everything. I'll...I'll let you know if there's any news.''

Dismayingly, tears were stinging her eyes, and she swung away from him, but his fingers closed about her arm and he turned her to him, tipping her chin with one hand.

''Don't!'' she choked, but he had his arm about her, hauling her close, letting her rest her head on his shoulder while she cried against him.

After a while she pulled away. ''Sorry.'' She wiped at her cheeks with the back of one hand.

''You needn't be,'' he assured her. ''How about I make you a hot drink while you get ready for bed?''

The suggestion was overwhelmingly tempting. Fifteen minutes later she was sitting on her bed with a light cotton robe over her nightdress when he tapped on the door and brought in a milky drink of cocoa.

He waited while she drank it, and then said, ''I'll kip on one of the sofas. You shouldn't be alone, and I don't suppose you want to rouse anyone at this time of the morning.''

''You've done enough—''

His reply was crisp, decisive. ''Only what any friend would. I'm staying until morning.''

In case her father took a turn for the worse.

''I'll be downstairs.'' He was already halfway to

the door, and she didn't have the energy to protest anymore.

"We have a spare bedroom," she said, giving in. "I'll get you some sheets—"

"You won't do anything except climb into bed," he said as she made a sluggish movement. "I'll find them. That cupboard in the hall?"

"Yes."

"Okay. Good night, Alysia."

When she woke several hours later it was light. She struggled out of bed, snatched up the wrap and went quietly down the stairs to her father's study to call the hospital.

As she put down the phone there was a sound in the doorway, and she turned to find Chase shrugging into a shirt. The button of his pants was undone but he'd closed the zip. His cheeks and chin were shadowed and his hair looked as though he'd rough-combed it with his fingers.

"How is he?"

Her voice husky, she replied, "Stable. I can see him anytime, and they may move him to a ward later today." She discovered that her legs were shaking.

"That's good."

He came forward, and without even thinking about it she went to meet him, stepping into his arms. Her cheek rested against warm, bare skin where his shirt was open, and she felt his breath on her temple as he bent his head. "Feel better now?"

"Heaps," she said on a thankful sigh.

"Did you sleep?"

"A bit." She lifted her head and tried to ease away. "I'm sorry if I woke you."

"I was awake." He still held her lightly. The skin

about his eyes crinkling, he said, "Do you know how luscious you look in the morning?"

Alysia had endured a late, anxious night, and before leaving the bedroom hadn't even run a brush over her hair. Sure that she looked far from luscious, she placed her hands on his arms and pushed free. "Don't tease."

"I wasn't. But I don't suppose," he added ruefully, feeling the stubble on his jaw with one hand, "that I'm much of a turn-on for any woman at the moment."

She might have told him he looked drop-dead sexy. It shocked her slightly that the rush of pleasure she'd experienced when she turned from the phone was partly due to him standing there with his shirt half-on, added to the overwhelming relief that her father's condition had improved. But there were more urgent things to think of. "I have to get dressed," she said, "and go back to the hospital."

"I'll make you some breakfast."

"I can't ask you to—"

"You've asked for nothing, Alysia. You need to eat."

Seeing that protest would be useless, Alysia said, "Thank you—toast and tea will do fine."

When she returned, dressed in a light blouse and skirt and flat-heeled shoes, Chase had a pile of toast on the table, and he slid two fried eggs onto a plate and set it in front of her at the table. "Get that down."

"I can't eat two!" she told him.

He sat down opposite her and took a piece of toast. "If you really don't want two I'll eat one."

He'd fastened his shirt except for the top two but-

tons and tucked it into his trousers, but was still un-
shaven. She dragged her gaze away from him and
concentrated on her breakfast, sliding one egg over
onto his plate.

As they shared a pot of tea Alysia said, "You could
use Dad's electric razor if you like. I wonder if I
ought to take it to the hospital."

"He might want it when he's feeling better."
Chase emptied his cup and put it down. "I'll whip
upstairs and use it now. Shall I drive you down?"

"No, I'll be fine. The shaver will be in Dad's en
suite. The end room. Chase—I'm truly grateful."
He'd been a rock last night, but showing her a gentler
side that she hadn't suspected in him.

He leaned back in his chair, regarding her with an
odd little smile. "It's nothing. Leave the dishes. I'll
deal with them and then be on my way. The front
door locks when you close it?"

"Yes." She was already pushing away her chair.
"I know my father will appreciate—"

"Forget it. And tell him I'll deal with the paper."

Maybe he was looking forward to it. A mean
thought. Guiltily she dismissed it.

She stayed with her father most of the morning and
promised to visit again in the evening.

In the corridor she ran into Sandra Ropata in her
white uniform. "Alysia! I'm sorry about your father.
I just came on duty and heard about it."

"Thanks, Sandra. He's looking a bit better."

"I'm sure he'll be all right. Look, I have to run."
Sandra touched her arm. "But try not to worry. He's
being well looked after."

Warmed by the brief encounter, Alysia returned to
her car and drove to the *Clarion* offices.

Chase rose from behind a desk cluttered with files, clippings and odd bits of paper, and removed a pile of newspapers from a chair so that she could sit down. "Spencer still improving?" he asked, and when she answered yes, he leaned back against the desk with folded arms. "And sent a lot of messages for me, did he?"

Alysia laughed a little. "How did you know?"

"I know Spencer."

"Not many messages, really." She relayed them.

"All in hand. I'll see him later if they let me."

Spencer's secretary tapped on the half-open door. "Sorry to interrupt," Glenys Heath looked strained, her lined, pleasant face almost haggard under graying curls, "but could you sign these, Chase?"

As he did so, the secretary turned to Alysia and enquired about Spencer, smiling with obvious relief that he seemed to be on the mend. "Oh, thank God! Will he be allowed visitors? I mean, apart from family."

"They said Chase could come today because Dad's fretting about the paper. But he needs to rest."

"I understand." But she looked disappointed.

Chase handed back the letters. "I'm sure he'll be asking to see you soon, Glenys."

When she had gone, he asked Alysia, "Have you had lunch?"

Over sandwiches and coffee in the staff cafeteria he said, "Will you be all right in that house on your own?"

"Of course."

"Did your father get a proper catch on that bathroom window?" he enquired. "And the other windows?"

"It isn't necessary." She'd never mentioned it.

Chase frowned. "I'd say it is. Do you have a friend you could move in with temporarily, or who could stay with you? Maybe the housekeeper wouldn't mind..."

"Mrs. Pearson's on holiday, and anyway she doesn't work at night. She has a family."

"I'll talk to your father," he said, "and arrange some proper security precautions."

"You're not to mention it!" She didn't want anything to interfere with Spencer's swift recovery.

Chase put down the sandwich in his hand. "You don't give the orders round here."

"My father does! And in his absence—"

"In his absence, I do."

"This is nothing to do with the *Clarion*—"

"True." His voice hardened. "It's to do with the fact that you've been coddled and spoiled and protected all your life, and consequently you can't believe that anything bad could happen to you."

Alysia bridled at the unexpected attack. "But—"

Chase didn't wait for her objection. "We're printing a report today about a girl who was attacked in broad daylight, walking down her own street to her own home. It can happen to anyone. Spencer's well-known in this town. His illness can't be kept secret. And that makes the house—and you—a possible target."

"You're trying to frighten me."

"I'm trying to point out to you that most of us live in the real world, not some ivory tower of privilege. And that you'd better wake up to it."

Alysia's eyes flashed. "Doesn't it get heavy, that

great big chip on your shoulder?'' she challenged him.

For a moment temper blazed in his face. Then he reached out and took one of her hands, his tone changing. ''It's only sensible to take elementary precautions. Your father would want it.''

Alysia wavered. A couple of times Spencer had mentioned that they ought to install better security. It had been all too easy for Chase to find an entry the night she'd left her keys behind.

Chase released her hand. ''I can get someone out there this afternoon. We needn't bother your father at this stage. Is he likely to object to the cost?''

Reluctantly she conceded, ''Not if he thought it was necessary.''

''Leave it to me, then. You'd better go home and get some rest. Someone needs to be there when the security firm comes to do the job.''

In the afternoon two men arrived at the house, and were soon busy fitting catches and deadlocks. As soon as they left, Alysia drove to the hospital.

Spencer was still tired. Chase came in a few minutes after her and gave his employer a brief account of how matters stood at the paper.

''He's a good lad,'' Spencer said rather breathlessly when Chase had left. ''Knows what he's doing.''

Alysia didn't stay much longer. She could see that trying to make conversation tired him.

At the house she vacuumed up shavings of wood and metal before making herself an early tea, then watched television for a while. She was preparing for bed when the phone shrilled.

She dashed into the hall in her nightgown and lifted the receiver. "Yes?"

"Have you been running?" Chase enquired.

Alysia slumped against the wall. "Oh, it's you."

"You were expecting someone else?"

"I thought maybe the hospital—"

"Sorry, I didn't mean to scare you."

"I'm fine. What did you want, Chase?"

"Just checking. Have you locked up properly?"

"Yes, I was going to bed." Alysia straightened away from the wall, absently winding the coiled cord of the telephone about her fingers.

"Sure you don't want company for the night?"

"No, thank you. The new locks look very secure."

"Okay," he said. "Good night, Princess."

Alysia put down the telephone slowly. It had been comforting last night knowing that Chase was just down the passageway. The house might be safe now, but suddenly it felt very lonely.

Even more so the following day, when Mrs. Pearson phoned in distress to say the family had been involved in a car accident on the way back from their holiday. She had a broken leg and one of the children was in hospital in Rotorua with multiple fractures. "She'll be all right, but it could take months before she's back to normal. I'm staying with my brother down here until she comes out of hospital. I'm sorry to let Mr. Kingsley down—"

"He'll understand," Alysia assured her. "Do let me know if there's any way we can help."

She must find something to send to the child, she reminded herself, and maybe flowers for the mother and presents for the other children, too. They'd been through a traumatic experience.

"We'll be all right," Mrs. Pearson said sturdily. "We've got lots of family down here."

After four days Spencer was pronounced out of danger. "We'll keep him a bit longer, and he should stay off work for a few weeks," the doctor told Alysia, "and then ease himself in gradually. He shouldn't drive. And the hospital dietitian will give you a diet sheet."

The next evening Alysia found that Chase was at the hospital before her. He rose from his chair, offering to leave, but Spencer insisted he stay. "We're almost finished," he told her. "Find yourself a magazine or something." He turned back to Chase to continue their discussion.

A couple of magazines sat on the broad sill of the big windows, but instead of picking one up Alysia stared with aching eyes at the panoramic view of the town.

The *Clarion* building that had once dominated now jostled for prominence with newer office blocks. Even though Spencer was the last male Kingsley, the name would live on in streets and parks honoring family members, in scholarships and endowments. The east wing of the hospital had been named for his mother.

Spencer soon began to flag, his eyelids drooping heavily, and Alysia and Chase left together. As they traversed the polished corridor Chase said, "After this, your father will need to lighten his workload. Has he mentioned what he intends to do?"

Rather dryly she said, "I can't see him relinquishing control, if that's what you're asking."

There was a slight pause before he said, his voice

so even it was almost expressionless, "I'm doing two jobs right now—mine and his. It would help if I knew how long it might last."

That was something she ought to have realized. "If I can do anything—"

"You?"

"I am supposed to work at the *Clarion* this year," she reminded him. "Even if you don't need a junior reporter, and haven't time to train one, maybe you can do with someone for filing or coffee-making..."

"You'd be prepared to do that?" he queried skeptically.

"If it's any help. I can use a computer too. And I majored in business administration. Wouldn't that be useful?"

They stopped to wait for the elevator. Chase pushed the button, then stared at her. "I thought you did a B.A."

"Did you?" she asked coolly. "Why?"

"I suppose I assumed..."

He had probably assumed a lot of things about her. "I have a business degree," she said crisply.

Chase rubbed a finger thoughtfully over his chin. "You realize you're hopelessly overqualified for what you're suggesting?"

"It's my family's business." That was exactly why she'd gained those qualifications, so that when she took over she'd be capable of doing the job. But as yet she lacked enough experience.

Chase looked at her curiously. "What I need is..."

"Yes?"

"Well, you could call it an editorial assistant," he decided. "It really means—"

"I know—dogsbody, gofer."

"Near enough." Chase smiled faintly.

The elevator doors glided open and they stepped in. "Glenys has been great," Chase said, selecting the ground floor, "but her knowledge and experience are wasted on routine tasks that anyone with a bit of intelligence could do. You must know something about the *Clarion,* even though we've hardly seen you in the building."

It almost sounded like a question. Alysia bit her lip momentarily, staring at the rapidly descending floor numbers without speaking.

The elevator stopped and when the doors slid apart Chase said, "I'll see you to your car."

As they left the building a cool breeze caught at the skirt of her short-sleeved dress and made her shiver slightly.

"You're cold." Chase put an arm around her and rubbed at the gooseflesh on her skin as they walked in silence across the tarseal. It made her feel extraordinarily...cherished.

There were few other people about and the lights that had come on at the edge of the parking area cast eerie shadows.

Chase waited while she unlocked the car. Then he opened the door for her. Alysia turned to thank him and found him closer than she'd expected.

Perhaps the sallow cast of his skin was caused by the lights, but that didn't explain the beard-shadow on his slightly hollowed cheeks, or the lines of strain etched about his eyes. She said, "You look tired."

"I've been burning some midnight oil."

She knew that. "Let me help," she urged again. "I can start tomorrow."

The pause lengthened. He nodded. "See you in the morning, then, eight-thirty? Come straight to my office."

Chapter Six

Next morning Alysia turned up early at the *Clarion* building and made her way upstairs.

Chase was sitting at his desk in his shirtsleeves and looked as though he'd already been working for some time.

"When did you arrive?" she asked him.

Chase glanced at his watch. "Couple of hours ago." He looked over her dark skirt and plain though elegant blouse with a mixture of amusement and approval. "I've organized a desk for you."

Alysia nodded. "I'll be working here?"

"There's room. That's the beauty of old buildings, nice big work spaces. And if you're going to assist me it's the handiest arrangement. Do you know your way around? If I give you a message will you know where to deliver it?"

"I remember the general layout, but there were changes when they installed the new computer systems and the color printing press."

"I'll show you around later," Chase promised.

Spencer's secretary came in, casting a curious glance at her.

"Good morning, Glenys," Chase said. "Alysia's going to help us out while her father's in hospital."

Glenys gave her a surprised, doubtful smile. "Oh. That's nice." She turned to Chase, presenting a sheaf of folders for his attention.

When he'd dealt with them, Chase spent an hour taking Alysia through the various departments.

In the print room Verne Hastie came up to them with a broad smile on his florid face, saying, "Well, looky who's arrived! It's years since we've seen you down here, Allie."

"Alysia," she said.

Verne's smile widened still further. "Never did like having her name shortened," he told Chase. "Even when she was a kid." He winked. "Little Miss High and Mighty, we called her."

"Did you?" Chase murmured.

Alysia was sure if she turned to look at him she'd see laughter in his eyes. She clamped her mouth shut.

"Alysia's going to be my assistant while her father's in hospital," Chase said. "She's refamiliarizing herself with the place. You don't mind if we just walk around?"

"Be my guests," Verne invited expansively. "But she knows her way around pretty well. Don't you, Allie? Oops! Alysia!" He grinned at her again.

Chase put a hand on Alysia's waist and steered her away. She hoped he couldn't feel her trembling.

One of the older men working the machines said, "Nice to see you here again, Alysia. We've missed you."

A very young-looking girl carrying a stack of paper that looked too big for her said, "Hello—I met you at the Christmas party."

Alysia smiled. "Yes, I remember...Franny?"

"That's right." The girl beamed back at her.

Alysia was glad when they went back upstairs. Chase paused at the coffee machine in the corridor to pour two coffees for them.

In his office Alysia took the chair he indicated.

He leaned against the edge of his desk and regarded her thoughtfully. "I didn't know you'd ever spent much time here."

"Not since I was a child." She used to love to come down and talk to everyone. And the presses had fascinated her.

"Why not?"

"I grew up," she said abruptly. "Anyway, the staff were busy and they didn't want me hanging about and making a nuisance of myself."

A line appeared between Chase's black brows. "Your father's words?" he asked slowly.

It was a good guess. Alysia shrugged.

Chase finished his coffee, not pressing her. "You can deal with a spreadsheet?" He crossed to a wheeled computer desk that had appeared in a corner of the big office. "Are you familiar with this program?"

Alysia followed him, peering at the screen. "An earlier version. I suppose this one won't be all that different."

He fished in a drawer. "Handbook," he said, placing it on the desk. "If you don't understand anything ask me or Glenys. This is what I want you to do..." He explained briefly, scribbling notes for her as he talked. She was mesmerized by his hands—capable hands, almost workmanlike hands, that could be hard yet gentle.

"Got that?"

She blinked, sitting upright. "I think so."

"Right, take your time. You'll soon pick it up."

By lunchtime she'd twice had to ask Chase to elucidate on points in the handbook, and appealed for his help again when she found it impossible to fit the requisite number of columns onto the screen. But she'd got quite a lot done. He seemed to approve.

They lunched in the cafeteria. After twenty minutes Chase scooped up his coffee and said, "I'm going back to my office. You're entitled to an hour if you want it."

"I'll come too." She hastily collected her own coffee and stood up to follow him.

Howard, sitting at a nearby table, called, "Don't let him slave-drive you, Allie."

Chase told her, "You don't have to come."

"I want to." She smiled at Howard.

"You don't mind him calling you Allie?" Chase queried as they left the big room.

"Howard's almost an uncle to me. He's known me forever."

"Like one of the family?" She fancied he was mentally capitalizing the last word.

"Something like that."

"So you're assisting Chase," Spencer said.

"He had so much to do with you being away. Your secretary looks tired, too. She and Chase have both been working extra hours."

Spencer frowned and cleared his throat. "Glenys is a good worker and very loyal."

Glenys Heath used her married name, but she'd separated years ago from an abusive husband. Alysia supposed that eventually she'd divorced him.

Once the husband had turned up at the *Clarion* offices, embarrassing her and setting the staff agog. Alysia hadn't been there but she'd heard from several sources that her father had shielded Glenys from him while someone called the police. Later the husband had left town. Alysia guessed that Glenys had never stopped feeling grateful to her employer for rescuing her. She'd repaid him with years of faithful, efficient and uncomplaining service.

"The staff all sent their regards," she told Spencer. They had clubbed in for a huge basket of flowers and fruit. "Why didn't you tell me your doctor had warned you to ease up?" She'd only found that out after his admission to hospital.

"Nothing you could do," Spencer said shortly, "except worry."

"Is that why you needed a deputy?"

He didn't answer her directly. "Chase seems to be doing a good job." He almost sounded as though he resented it.

When the hospital phoned a few days later to say Spencer was being discharged, Alysia went to his room to find fresh clothes for him to wear.

On the mahogany dressing table her mother used to keep a narrow crystal vase filled with flowers. After the funeral Alysia had gone in to the room and found a posy of dead pansies, the bottom of the vase dry and stained. She'd taken it away, washed it and filled it with miniature roses and green fern. As she was replacing it her father came in.

"What are you doing here?" he'd asked, his voice unnaturally harsh.

"I picked some flowers for you," she said. "Because Mum isn't here to do it anymore." Her voice sank as she struggled not to cry.

At the expression in his eyes she cringed, afraid he was going to be angry. Then he looked at the fresh blooms and said tiredly, "You're a good girl, Alysia. But don't do it again. Your mother's gone. You can't take her place."

The vase was still there, clean and empty. Everything else that was personal of her mother's had been disposed of. Spencer had given Alysia the silver brush and comb set, and she'd asked for a couple of pieces of jewelry that she specially liked. He'd put the rest aside for when she was older, and presented them to her on her eighteenth birthday.

She found underwear and socks, a tie, then went to the wardrobe for trousers, a shirt and a sports jacket. Laying the clothing on the bed she said aloud, "Shoes."

Two neat rows of shoes sat on the floor of the wardrobe. She stooped to pick up a pair of black slip-ons, and her eye was caught by a fall of deep pink satin almost touching the floor.

Pink satin? Blinking, she straightened, and without thought pushed aside the hangers to reveal a long feminine robe edged with lace.

Aunt Patricia had cleared her mother's wardrobe and given everything to the Salvation Army in Auckland. Spencer hadn't wanted to see anyone in Waikura walking down the street in his wife's clothes.

Had this garment some special significance, that he'd kept it all these years?

Or, if it wasn't her mother's…

Feeling like a guilty intruder, she shoved the hangers into place and hastily closed the door.

Spencer reluctantly obeyed medical advice not to return immediately to work, but when Alysia offered to stay home he reacted irascibly. "They wouldn't have discharged me if I needed twenty-four-hour care. You're more use at the office," he grumbled. "Chase says you're doing quite well, shaping up nicely."

She contented herself with leaving him a nourishing lunch and phoning a couple of times a day.

"When he comes back," Chase asked her, "do you want to shift to the newsroom?"

Unaccountably, Alysia's heart seemed to contract. She enjoyed working alongside Chase. She'd learned a lot, and liked being involved at the level where the decisions were made. Even though she wasn't making them, Chase occasionally surprised her by asking for her opinion.

"That's what my father planned," she reminded him.

For a moment he looked slightly irritated. "If you really wanted to be a reporter I'd have thought you would have asked your father for a holiday job while you were at university."

"I always knew there was a job for me after I'd qualified," she said evasively.

Then Glenys came bustling in with some papers for Chase, and Alysia thankfully returned to her computer.

No further mention was made of moving Alysia to

the newsroom, until one day Chase sent her to deliver a message to one of the reporters.

The woman she wanted wasn't there, but the sole occupant, one of the *Clarion's* longtime male employees, told her, "Hang about and she'll probably turn up."

Alysia was perched on an empty desk chatting to the man when Chase put his head around the door and said, "I need someone to cover a high school board meeting tonight." Seeing the lone reporter, he added, "Looks like you just volunteered, Pete."

The man groaned. "Come off it, Chase. We don't cover those things. The secretary sends in a report if anything interesting happens, and if there's space we shove in a couple of paragraphs."

"I just got a phone call from a disgruntled parent, and there might be a real story in it."

"I promised I'd take my wife to a film she's been dying to see and it's the last night it's on. She'll kill me. We arranged a baby-sitter and everything."

Chase came into the room and switched his gaze to Alysia. He said abruptly, "What about you, then?"

"Me?" She slid off the desk.

"You want to be a reporter, don't you? Here's your chance." He held out a piece of paper. "That's the time and place. I want a report in the morning. Not more than five hundred words."

Next morning Alysia delivered a disk and a neat printout to Chase's desk. Then she took a pile of photographs to be filed in the library.

After that she rushed some late paper copy to the print room, escaping as quickly as she could while Verne Hastie was still grumbling about last-minute changes, and arrived back at her desk past midmorning.

Chase wasn't in, but when he did return the first thing he said was, "I told you that piece couldn't be longer than five hundred words."

She hadn't realized until then how much she'd hoped he would like it, say how good it was. Instinctively defensive, she said, "I know, but—"

"This—" he picked up her printed copy from his desk "—is nearer seven hundred."

"Six hundred and forty-four," she argued. "The argument's quite complex. You can make the space for it, can't you?"

"It was a school board meeting, Alysia! The fate of the community doesn't hinge on it."

"*You* said there might be a real story in it. Well, I gave you a real story!"

"Didn't they tell you at journalism school about the importance of word lengths?"

"I needed the length to do justice to the issues."

Chase looked at her, and her heart skipped a beat because his eyes were hard. Then he shrugged, seeming to make an effort to relax. "I guess you couldn't make it shorter." But just as she began to feel good about her victory, he added, "The sub-ed will fix it."

"*Fix* it?"

His eyes were cool, daring her to object. "That's her job. If you can't get it right, she'll do it for you. Only next time, try harder."

She knew it was the sub-editor's job, but she was still smarting. "I'd like to see *you* try," she muttered, turning away to hide her disappointment.

"Come here."

"What?" She turned warily at the quiet command.

"I said, come here." It was definitely an order. Chase sat down at his desk and pulled the report toward him. Then he picked up a pencil. "Stand there," he said, indicating a position beside him.

A stroke of the pencil, then another. A phrase crossed out. When he lined out an entire paragraph, she almost protested. Then he wrote in a short sentence that said exactly the same thing. Alysia bit her lip.

"And this," Chase said, circling another paragraph, "would be better up here." He drew a line up the page. "Then you wouldn't need this." The pencil slashed across another passage.

When he'd finished he pushed the pages toward her. She had asked for a lesson and she'd got it. "Thank you," she said, torn between chagrin and admiration of his skill. "I guess I could learn a lot from you."

Chase shoved back his chair and looked up at her with narrowed eyes. "I'm giving you fair warning—that's the last time I make concessions for the boss's daughter. Time you learned to swim with the rest of us, Princess."

"I never asked for special concessions," she reminded him, thrusting out her chin. "You can bawl me out anytime you feel the need."

"I've lost the urge for today." He actually smiled at her. "Basically you did a good job."

Alysia began to move away, but was unable to resist. "Did I really?"

"For a beginner. I might even trust you with another assignment."

* * *

Within weeks Spencer was back in his office, but he tired easily and usually asked Alysia to take him home well before five.

Mrs. Pearson had reluctantly given notice so that she could concentrate her energies on her daughter's rehabilitation.

"I suppose I'll have to find someone else," Spencer complained.

"Do we need anyone?" Alysia queried. "Maybe a weekly cleaner, but I prefer to do the cooking myself." It ensured his diet was a healthy one.

Spencer was doubtful but relieved. "Can you manage?"

"If it doesn't work out we'll look for a replacement," Alysia suggested.

Chase often came to the house after hours, and while the men were deep in discussion Alysia cooked extra food and then called them both to the table. One evening he arrived as she was standing on the front step, talking to a neighbor who had delivered a bag of home-grown tomatoes.

"I'm glad your father's feeling better," the man said, declining her invitation to come in. He nodded to Chase and went off down the driveway.

Alysia stepped back to let Chase in, and a large, almost heart-shaped tomato dropped from the bag and rolled to the step.

He stooped and picked it up, inspecting it. "Doesn't look any the worse for wear." He grinned at her, his thumb rubbing at the firm red flesh. "They used to call them love apples."

A strange sensation attacked her midriff, a sort of breathless longing as she watched him cupping the tomato, almost caressing it.

He replaced it in the top of the bag and she steadied it, finding the smooth skin warm from his hand.

"Actually we've got plenty of tomatoes." She hoped her voice sounded normal. "But people have been so helpful and nice since Dad's heart attack..."

"There are some nice people in this town."

"Is that why you've stayed here for so long?"

He glanced at her. "No," he said.

"There must be a reason." She preceded him down the passageway.

"There is." He sounded curt.

Alysia turned her head and looked at him curiously. "If you're as good as my father says, you could be working for a big city paper."

"Maybe."

"Did you think you couldn't make it?" she asked with conscious provocation, wanting a real reaction from him, not these noncommittal replies.

He looked at her again. "What do *you* think?"

"That maybe you prefer to be a big fish in a little pond."

"You don't think I'd make it as a bigger fish in a big pond?"

She hadn't a doubt of it. And surely that was what he must want, ultimately—to move on, and upward. Alysia fought a strange sense of loss, almost panic. Spencer needed him now. She stopped walking and turned to him. "You won't leave my father in the lurch?"

"No," he said, "I wouldn't do that." His hand briefly touched her cheek. "Don't worry about it."

Maybe she'd sounded pathetic. She hadn't meant to. Straightening her spine, she said, "My father's on the terrace. You know the way. I'll just put these in the kitchen.''

On the morning of Alysia's twenty-second birthday her father placed a small parcel by her plate at breakfast.

Pulling off the wrappings, she found a flat, oblong box, and opened the lid on a single row of milky, lustrous pearls. ''They're real?''

''Of course.''

''It's lovely.'' Not for anything would she have revealed that she'd have preferred something that she might have worn casually without worrying about its value. She got up and went to kiss his cheek.

''Look after that,'' he unnecessarily advised her. ''Pearls are a good investment.''

Alysia spent the afternoon preparing for the party Spencer had insisted she must have. Now that he had a resident hostess he seemed eager to entertain whenever an opportunity offered. He'd told her he'd pay for something new and pretty for her to wear, but she'd used her *Clarion* wages to buy a dark-rose strapless dress with a soft, floating skirt.

Chase handed Alysia a gift-wrapped package. She opened it up and found, nestled in tissue, a tiny fairytale castle of crystal with gold spires.

''It's beautiful!'' she exclaimed, enchanted.

''I'm glad you like it.''

''But you weren't supposed to—'' The invitations had specified no gifts.

''I just happened to see it, and I thought of you.''

''Well, thank you, it's exquisite.''

When, later, he asked Alysia to dance, she said, ''I thought you might bring Mariette tonight.'' She'd

"I haven't seen her lately."

"Oh." She tried hard to sound disappointed for him. The little skip of gladness in her heart wasn't appropriate. "I suppose you've been too busy to make the trip to Auckland." Alysia reminded herself it wasn't her fault her father had suffered a heart attack, and Chase had assumed the extra workload. He'd wanted the deputy editor's job and taking over in an emergency was part of it. "She could have visited you."

"Mariette finds Waikura rather boring."

"Even with you here?"

Chase gave a small laugh. "Are you paying me a compliment, Alysia?"

"Does she pay you compliments?"

His eyes gleamed down at her. "Far from it, last time we spoke. I think that's died a natural death." He didn't seem to mind too much. "What about you?" he asked.

"What about me?"

"Spencer said you have friends here from Auckland. Anyone special?"

"They're all special. That's one of them, there. Donna." She indicated the pretty blonde dancing in the arms of a young man in a pink shirt. "I'll introduce you if you like."

Chase returned his gaze to her, the gleam in the dark depths intensifying. "Thanks," he said rather dryly. "But I don't think she's my type."

"You go for brunettes, don't you?"

His brows rose.

"Otherwise, how can you tell that Donna isn't your type just by looking at her?"

"She's too young."

"The same age as me," Alysia pointed out.

A rather complicated expression flitted over his face. "Is that so?" he said finally.

Did he think she was hinting or something? Hastily she changed the subject. "Thank you again for my castle. Where did you find it, if you haven't been to Auckland lately?"

"Right here in town," he told her, with a faint, crooked smile. "It's surprising what you can find in Waikura. Even when you're not looking for it."

The music changed, and Chase folded her into his arms and their bodies moved in harmony.

His arms tightened and Alysia was overwhelmingly conscious of the hardness and warmth of him, the taut muscles of his thighs against hers.

Disturbed, she lifted her head and stared at him.

A smile touched his mouth. His eyes flared and she knew with certainty he was fully aware of her—as caught up in the spell of the music and sexual attraction as she was. The music came to an end, and for a fantastic moment she thought he wasn't going to let her go, but then his hands fell from her.

When they reached her father's side Spencer was smiling benignly. "Enjoying your party, Alysia?"

"It's a wonderful evening."

"Thank you for the dance," Chase said. "We must do it again sometime."

He wanted to do it again right now, and do a lot more besides, but there were numerous reasons for cooling his inconvenient desire to find the nearest bed and ravish her.

Spencer's fragile state and her resultant stress, the fact that she worked in Chase's office and he was several years younger than himself were complications he'd prefer not to deal with. Besides all that she was his employer's daughter and an heiress.

Suddenly, showing the local princess that she was no more special, no less carnal, than any other woman was both shallow and more than a little squalid. Alysia—the Alysia who had refused to leave her father's bedside although she was dropping with fatigue, who had stepped in to the breach to help out at the newspaper, who uncomplainingly carried out the most menial tasks, worked like the proverbial Trojan and went home to care for her ailing and consequently impatient father—*that* Alysia deserved better.

Better, maybe, than Chase Osborne.

Chapter Seven

Spencer continued to improve, but was still tired and often irritable. Alysia was tired and strung up, too.

Working with Chase every day didn't help. Since her party she'd found it increasingly difficult to hide her intense awareness of him. Even sitting at her desk with her back to him, she knew of his every movement, and at times she was sure he was watching her; she could feel his stare like a touch on her nape as she studied the computer screen.

But he treated her as if he were a sort of aloof elder brother, kind but distant. Alysia redoubled her efforts to appear mature and in control, doing her best to emulate Glenys Heath's brisk efficiency.

Chase gave her another assignment. Covering the cat show wasn't the story of the week but she got to take a photographer along, and this time she turned in a piece that was within the specified word length.

When the sub-editor cut it further, removing the

part she was most proud of, she swallowed her disappointment and shrugged it off.

"Today's news, tomorrow's garbage wrapping,"
she reminded herself.

As she was opening the office mail one morning
she found an invitation to the annual Chamber of
Commerce charity fund-raising dinner-dance.

She saw Chase glance at it, then toss it on the pile
to be discarded.

"You're not going?" she asked.

"Should I?"

"It's the sort of thing the deputy editor of the *Clarion* should be seen at." She knew her father would
think so.

Chase looked at her. "You'd know."

Unsure of his tone, she didn't answer. He picked
up the invitation again and seemed to study it before
looking up again. "Would you come with me?" He
threw the words out like a careless challenge.

"Me?" Alysia looked at him suspiciously. But she
supposed he was short of a partner. He'd hardly had
a social life since her father's illness.

The twinge of compunction she felt was unwar-
ranted. It was as much in his own interests as Spencer's that Chase had spent so much time on the job
and consequently lost his girlfriend.

Come to think of it, she hadn't had much social
life either lately. And recently Spencer had given
every indication of finding her constant watchfulness
an irritation. Maybe he'd welcome an evening alone.
"All right," she said. "I will."

The surprise in his eyes gave her a small burst of
satisfaction.

* * *

Alysia wore her rose-colored dress. The weather had cooled a little and she draped a light lambswool wrap about her shoulders.

"Have a good time." Spencer beamed as he waved them off. "I know Alysia is in safe hands."

They shared a table with two other couples. Chase belonged to the same squash club as the men, and Alysia discovered she'd been at school with one of the women. They found plenty to talk about, and when she was dancing she didn't feel the need to talk at all.

She and Chase seemed able to read each other's minds when they danced—or each other's body language. They advanced and retreated, touched and broke apart, locked eyes and exchanged wordless messages.

It didn't mean anything, Alysia told herself. It was all part of the dance.

But when the lights dimmed and the music became dreamy Chase pulled her into his arms and she laid her head on his shoulder, closing her eyes and breathing in the scent of him, warm and potent and very individually his.

He took her arm on the way to his car, and she could have sworn she felt his touch tingling in her toes. She'd had too much to drink, she warned herself, although she was far from drunk. Yet she was almost dizzy with a strange tension; her skin felt as though tiny sparks were igniting all over it.

She slid into the car when Chase opened the door for her, and she found her eyes following him as he walked to the driver's side. Biting her lip, she tried to force herself to some kind of sobriety.

She wrapped the lambswool about her shoulders,

and as he started the car Chase glanced at her. "Cold?"

"A bit." But the shivery feelings encompassing her body had nothing to do with being cold.

He switched on the heater. Alysia gazed at his hands on the wheel, noticing how his long fingers gripped it, how strong they looked.

When he drew up outside the house she said, "Thank you, Chase. I had a great time."

He turned to face her, one arm resting on the steering wheel. "Would I be pushing my luck if I kissed you good-night?"

She ought to make some light remark, but as her eyes lowered they found his mouth, curved in a slight smile, and she remembered how it felt on hers—firm and sure and erotic. Her lips parted and the tip of her tongue momentarily moistened the lower one. "I—"

He didn't wait for her to finish. Which was just as well because she didn't know what she was going to say. His hand tipped her chin and he leaned forward and kissed her, coaxing her lips open.

She held her breath, and then let it escape with a sigh into his mouth, and his arm came around her. Pulling her close, he shifted their positions so that her head fell back, and her breasts were crushed against his chest.

Chase's fingers drifted to her throat, making small exploratory movements on her skin, and he brushed aside the fine wool that covered her shoulders so that he could find the bare skin there, right to the edge of her dress.

His hand slid under her arm, pausing when his thumb found the softness at the side of her breast, stroking it gently before moving on to delicately out-

The Silhouette Reader Service™ — Here's how it works:

Accepting your 2 free books and gift places you under no obligation to buy anything. You may keep the books and gift and return the shipping statement marked "cancel." If you do not cancel, about a month later we'll send you 6 additional books and bill you just $3.15 each in the U.S., or $3.50 each in Canada, plus 25¢ shipping & handling per book and applicable taxes if any.* That's the complete price and — compared to cover prices of $3.99 each in the U.S. and $4.50 each in Canada — it's quite a bargain! You may cancel at any time, but if you choose to continue, every month we'll send you 6 more books, which you may either purchase at the discount price or return to us and cancel your subscription.

*Terms and prices subject to change without notice. Sales tax applicable in N.Y. Canadian residents will be charged applicable provincial taxes and GST.

Play The

Lucky Hearts Game

and get...

FREE BOOKS & a FREE GIFT... YOURS to KEEP!

Scratch Here!
then look below to see
what your cards get you...

Yes! I have scratched off the silver card.
Please send me my **2 FREE BOOKS**
and **FREE GIFT**. I understand that I am under
no obligation to purchase any books as
explained on the back of this card.

DETACH AND MAIL CARD TODAY! (S-R-03/02)

© 1998 HARLEQUIN ENTERPRISES LTD. ® and TM are
trademarks owned by Harlequin Books S.A., used under license

315 SDL DH4C   **215 SDL DH4A**

NAME   (PLEASE PRINT CLEARLY)

ADDRESS

APT.#   CITY

STATE/PROV.   ZIP/POSTAL CODE

Twenty-one gets you   Twenty gets you   Nineteen gets you   **TRY AGAIN!**
2 FREE BOOKS and   **2 FREE BOOKS!**   **1 FREE BOOK!**
a **FREE GIFT!**

Offer limited to one per household and not valid to current
Silhouette Romance® subscribers. All orders subject to approval.

line her shoulder blades and then drift over her back.
And all the time his mouth continued its subtle assault
on hers.

She felt the small tug as he discovered the hook
holding the fastening of her dress, and heard the rasp
of the zip. Stirring, she pulled away, and he turned
his head, his lips feathering her cheek. "Just your
back," he murmured. "I want to feel your skin...it's
so smooth...beautiful." His hand was already trailing
down her spine, his fingers on the delicate indenta-
tions. He found her mouth again with his, and this
time the kiss was deep and heart-stopping, as his hand
splayed against her back.

Then it traveled swiftly upward to her nape and he
broke the kiss, breathing hard. He pressed his mouth
to the side of her neck, to her shoulder, and his fingers
fumbled for the zip and closed it. He buried a hand
in her hair and kissed her again, and then his cheek
was against hers and he muttered in her ear, "We'd
better break this party up before it goes any further..."

Alysia was breathing unevenly, too, her head singing and her blood racing. She bit on her lower lip,
trying to dispel the fog of desire that held her.

Chase reached across and opened her door, then
pushed open his own and was beside her by the time
she'd got out. He shoved his fingers through his hair
and looked down at her.

He touched her cheek with the back of his hand
and then took her arm lightly, steering her toward the
door.

Still dazed, she let herself in to the house and tip-
toed up to bed, relieved that her father wasn't around.

For a long time she lay awake, wondering if Chase was doing the same thing.

He wasn't in bed but he was awake, staring out the window of the warehouse apartment he'd rented in the center of town. From there he could see the hill across the river, pick out which lights probably belonged to the Kingsley mansion.

What the hell was he getting himself into here? Making love to Alysia Kingsley was playing with fire in more ways than he cared to count. Hadn't he already decided to leave her strictly alone? He'd successfully put some distance between them at work, absolutely necessary if he wasn't to give in to a disastrous, insane desire to grab her, throw her across a desk and kiss her senseless—at least. He'd kept their relationship strictly neutral, only to have his resolution crumble at the mere suggestion that she might welcome an invitation.

He'd expected her to slap him down when he'd asked if she'd come with him tonight. Once she'd said yes he couldn't back out. And after holding her in his arms on the dance floor he'd not been able to resist asking for more.

That was the trouble, he told himself. He always wanted more. The story of his life.

But although she'd been hesitant, a little nervous, so had she...

"How was your evening?" Alysia's father enquired at breakfast. Still in her dressing gown, she was serving him toast and a poached egg.

"Fine," she answered automatically.

"Chase looked after you all right?"

Against her will she felt heat rise in her cheeks. "Of course. We had a good time."

He nodded, apparently satisfied, and attacked the egg. "Don't we have any bacon?"

"It's bad for you. Too fatty. You shouldn't have too many eggs, either. "

"Hmmph." Spencer scowled. "You ought to get out and about more. I told Chase, sitting around home with me won't do you any good. Glad he took the hint."

The flush died into a chill stillness. "Hint?"

Spencer glanced at her and seemed to realize he'd blundered. "Not that he needed much," he said hastily. "I believe the boy was afraid I wouldn't approve. All it wanted was a gentle push in the right direction."

Her direction. Alysia found herself clutching a fork like a weapon. She put it down carefully and looked at the perfectly poached egg reposing on a slice of toast before her. Nausea rose in her throat. "I wish you hadn't done that."

"You just told me you had a good time. No need to be coy."

"I'm not coy!"

Spencer seemed surprised and perhaps displeased at the passion in her voice. "Then don't be silly," he said. "You could do worse than Chase. He's going far, that young man."

"Far from Waikura, probably," Alysia said.

"What do you mean by that?"

"He won't be content here for much longer."

Maybe she shouldn't have said it while Spencer still needed Chase. But surely he must have considered the possibility? Her father was far from stupid.

"Hmm. That depends." Spencer sawed at the toast. "With the right incentives..."

The new promotion might keep him for a short while, but if he was still not satisfied—or not for long—what then?

What else would make the proposition of remaining with a provincial daily attractive to a newspaperman like Chase Osborne?

Shares in the company?

The paper was the only one in town and enjoyed a wide rural circulation. The shares must be solid.

Perhaps along with his recent promotion and a raise in salary Chase had secured other perks. He drove a fairly new car—not flashy but not cheap, either. "Does the *Clarion* pay for Chase's car?" she blurted.

Spencer looked at her in astonishment. "Chase's contract is confidential," he said shortly, pushing away his plate.

"It must be a good one."

Spencer scowled. "It is."

But if he got a better offer from a bigger paper, what further bait would Spencer have to hold out to keep him?

A fantastic thought brushed by, like a trailing cobweb, and she mentally shook it away.

On Monday morning Alysia dressed in a straight navy-blue skirt and a plain white blouse, and pinned her hair back, making sure no strand escaped from the neat knot secured with a flat black bow.

Before entering the office she took a deep breath and put on a calm, indifferent expression.

Chase was already at his desk. He pushed back his chair. "Good morning. You look very businesslike."

His eyes smiled, although she detected a hint of reserve.

"Thank you." Turning to her desk, she said crisply, "What do you want done this morning?"

There was a moment's silence. "There's a list by your computer. What's the matter, Alysia?"

She turned, relieved to find that he had halted by his own desk. "What do you mean?"

"You seemed to enjoy yourself on Saturday night." His eyes searched hers.

"I had a good time, I already told you. And you got your reward. Value for money, I'd say. Now, is this the list?" She picked up the piece of paper lying on her desk, willing her hand not to tremble.

Chase looked as though she'd hit him in the solar plexus. "Do you have to practice, or is it in your genes?" he asked her harshly.

"Sorry?" Alysia's expression was a combination of puzzlement and hauteur.

"The lady of the manor thing. Making sure the serfs don't get ideas above their station just because you chose to let your hair down once or twice."

"I'm not—"

One of the photographers tapped on the open door and walked in. "Those prints you asked for, Chase—oh! Am I interrupting?"

"I think we're finished—aren't we, Chase?" Alysia said pleasantly, running her eyes down the list in her hand. Let him think what he liked. It was better than having him imagine she needed his charity. "I'll go and fetch that stuff you want from stationery, first."

He met her bland stare, his eyes holding an angry dark fire. "I'll see you *later*," he promised, and turned to the photographer. "Show me what we've got."

But when Alysia next came into the office she found only a scribbled list of requests that she spent the rest of the day fulfilling. Glenys said Chase had been called away on some urgent business.

"What business?" Alysia queried involuntarily.

Glenys look surprised and a little disapproving. "He didn't say."

He turned up again just before the office closed for the day. "I thought you'd have taken your father home by now," he said.

"He insists he's all right, but I will soon." Crisply she detailed what she'd done, and he gave her a curt nod.

"Okay. You'd better get Spencer out of here."

She ought to be relieved that he'd decided to drop the subject of their date. Instead she wanted to cry. "Good night."

Sifting through some papers on his desk, Chase said remotely, "Try to persuade him to take a day off tomorrow. Maybe you should stay with him."

"Stay?"

He glanced up. "To make sure he rests. I'm sure we can manage without you."

In other words she wasn't really needed. Alysia felt as though he'd slapped her. She'd thought he'd begun to rely on her increasing expertise in the job. Now he could dismiss her, just like that?

Spencer returned to the office the following morning but took the afternoon off. Chase insisted Alysia stay with her father. They'd spent the morning being chillingly polite, talking only when necessary.

In the next few weeks things thawed only slightly. At work they were both very businesslike, hardly looking at each other. Whenever Chase called at the house Alysia took herself off to her room as soon as she decently could. Spencer asked her if they'd quarreled.

"Why should you think that?"

"You always disappear when Chase is here."

"We work in the same room all day. You can see too much of a person, you know."

Spencer frowned. "I don't want Chase to feel unwelcome here. I'd appreciate it if you'd stay in the same room next time, make the effort to be the good little hostess I know you can be."

Alysia swallowed a tart retort. Had Chase been complaining that she'd been inhospitable?

"And another thing," Spencer said. "You tend to disagree with everything he says. I hope you don't carry on like that at work."

She didn't, and partly because she was so scrupulous not to argue with him in the office, she often challenged him over the dining table. They'd had some fairly spirited debates, affording her more mental stimulation than she'd enjoyed since university. But they never allowed the discussion to descend to personal issues. "No, I don't," she said.

"Well, there's no need to do it here, either. You have a lively mind, but don't let it lead you into showing off. You could learn a lot if you just sat quietly and listened."

Alysia waited for a flash of irritation to subside. "Yes, Dad. I'll remember."

Next time Chase came she opened the door to him, smiled widely, and cooed, "Chase! How nice of you to call.'' It was only a couple of hours since she'd left the office, but she acted as if he was a welcome visitor whom she hadn't seen in ages.

His eyes narrowed, but before he could make any comment she was swaying down the wide hall ahead of him to push open the door of the lounge where her father was watching the TV news. ''Dad, Chase is here. Isn't that nice?'' She flashed another smile at Chase and said, ''You'll stay for dinner, won't you? Of course you will. I'll just pop another potato in the pot.''

Spencer said, ''Come in, Chase. About this latest upheaval in the government, maybe we could get hold of the local MP for an interview.''

Chase had no choice but to join Spencer while Alysia, with a smug little smile, returned to the kitchen.

She made sure the meal was superb, and when Chase complimented her she all but fluttered her lashes at him as she thanked him in a demure voice. Abetted by Spencer, she refused help with the clearing up, but appeared in the lounge later and gracefully took a seat near her father, apparently hanging on Chase's every word, and breathlessly agreeing with everything he said.

She saw the glint that appeared in his eyes, and after Spencer cast her a slightly baffled glance she toned down the act a trifle, but of course Chase wasn't fooled.

When he stood up to go he said, ''Don't get up, Spencer. Alysia, maybe you could walk me to the door?''

After playing the perfect hostess all evening she could hardly refuse. Alysia stood up reluctantly and he let her precede him to the lounge door, then pulled it shut behind him. She hurried to open the outer door and waited, but he took her outside with him, a hand on her arm, and pulled that door almost closed before stopping to look down at her. "Would you like to tell me what that was all about?" he asked grimly.

Pretending innocence was pointless. "Dad thought I hadn't been very welcoming to you lately."

He stared at her for a moment, and then his forbidding expression broke and he burst into laughter. "Well, you certainly pulled out all the stops tonight. I began to wonder if I'd strayed into the wrong house."

"I thought I did it quite well," she said, tossing her head. "You're not *still* complaining, are you?"

"I've never complained, Princess. Did you really think I had?"

She'd been too angry to think about it, but he wouldn't have. "Not really, I suppose."

"Given a choice," he said, "I think I'd rather be drowned in acid than smothered in sugar." His mouth twisted. "Either way, the message is loud and clear."

"Message?"

"That you're willing to knuckle under at work, take orders and advice from me. But in private you're strictly off-limits. Chase Osborne isn't nearly good enough for Spencer Kingsley's daughter."

Her eyes flew wide. "I never thought that!"

The lift of his brows told her he didn't believe her. "You walked in to my office the Monday after that Chamber of Commerce thing and looked at me as though I were some peasant who'd dared lay hands on a royal highness."

"I'm *not* that kind of snob!"

He smiled—after a fashion. "What sort of snob are you, then?"

"Not at all, I hope," she said stiffly. "You think you know all about the real world, but that *I'm* some spoiled, pathetic brat living in an ivory tower. I'm not. So you don't need to feel responsible for my social life. And—" the real grievance surfacing, she added almost viciously "—you don't have to do every damned thing my father says!"

The sort-of smile vanished. "I don't know what you're talking about."

"You asked me out because he suggested it to you."

"Actually I thought *you* suggested it. Something I should be seen at, you said."

"I said you should go! I wasn't looking for an invitation."

"Whatever," he said impatiently. "I don't need your father to tell me how to organize my life, Alysia."

"But he did say to you—"

"Whatever he said had nothing to do with it." He drew her into his arms and bent his head; his mouth closed over hers for a few seconds before he drew away. "That should tell you why I asked you," he said, his eyes smoldering.

She stared up at him and he kissed her again more deeply.

Her body automatically curved in to him, her mouth softening and parting under the tender insistence of his. She'd been starved for this, starved for the feel and the scent of him. She couldn't believe that they'd been side by side for weeks without falling together into this sweet abyss.

It was confusing feeling like this about a man she had once been sure she disliked.

Hearing a sound inside, she stirred, and he let her go.

"Tomorrow," he said. "Dinner?"

"I don't know..." she said longingly. "My father's been a bit breathless today."

"I'm sure Glenys would be happy to come and keep him company."

"We can't impose on her out of office hours."

Chase looked at her thoughtfully. "She's very fond of your father."

"She's been working for him a long time, but still..."

"See how he is tomorrow. We'll talk about it."

In the morning she felt nervous walking into the office. Chase looked up and smiled at her. "Hi."

"Hi." Alysia smiled jerkily back and paused in the doorway before moving to her own desk. She put down her bag and knew that Chase had risen to walk over and stand behind her.

She felt his thumb run up the back of her neck and his hand curved under her chin, turning her face up to him. Swiftly he bent and stole a quick kiss, then dropped his hand and moved away. "Now, Miss Kingsley, I have a meeting in a few minutes, and while I'm gone..."

Chapter Eight

All day Alysia bathed in the warm aftermath of that brief caress. Several times she found herself staring into space, wrapped in dreamy anticipation of the evening ahead.

Spencer didn't try to hide his delight. "You've been stuck at home for far too long. And I know what the two of you were up to last night when you went outside. You mustn't be touchy, Alysia. You'll always catch more flies with honey."

Alysia recalled what Chase had said about suffocating in sugar, and couldn't help laughing.

Spencer smiled. "It's nice to see you happy. Have a good time."

Alysia almost expected him to rub his hands together.

She did have a good time. She guarded her tongue, careful not to give Chase any excuse to accuse her again of snobbery. Chase too, although his eyes held the lazy amusement that often roused her to defensiveness, refrained from baiting her, the amusement gradually becoming a smoldering promise.

And they ended the evening in each other's arms, sharing long, spine-tingling kisses.

"Will your father be waiting up for you?" he asked her at last, his forehead resting against hers, his arms still loosely holding her.

"No. He goes to bed quite early these days. Do you want to come in...for coffee?"

They'd had coffee at the restaurant, but Chase said, "Yes."

He helped her out of the car and kept his arm around her waist while she let them in. As she made to slip away from his hold and head for the kitchen he turned her fully into his arms and began kissing her again, walking her backward toward the lounge.

When they reached it, she freed her mouth and laughingly enquired, "What about the coffee?"

"The hell with coffee." He swept her right off her feet, striding to the wide sofa and sinking down on it, capturing her mouth again with his.

Everyone at the *Clarion* soon knew the deputy editor was dating the boss's daughter.

Alysia felt almost drunk with a strange combination of desire, frustration, and mental and emotional stimulation. Just talking to Chase was as bracing as a walk in the wind, and he had only to look at her to make her skin hot and deliciously aware. When he took her in his arms she felt like a melting flame, and his hand on her breast or stroking her thigh burned her soul.

That he hadn't tried to make love to her fully she

put down to his knowing that Spencer wouldn't approve.

Sometimes she deliberately goaded him, wanting to know if his desire for her was stronger than his respect for her father. But each time he pushed her away in the end, dragging harsh breaths into his lungs, his voice thick as he said, "Enough, Alysia."

So all she ended up with was a load of intense frustration that left her sleepless for hours.

She knew that they couldn't go on like this. Something had to happen to either move their developing relationship along, or...

The *or* didn't bear thinking about.

And then her father had another heart attack.

Spencer's secretary had buzzed him for a visitor, and when he didn't answer she went in and found him slumped over his desk.

Glenys called an ambulance and Alysia traveled with her father to the hospital. Again she spent hours at his bedside, vaguely conscious that for much of the time Chase was with her, silently holding her hand. For once his presence was quiet and soothing, the acute, unsettling awareness between them muted by concern.

At dawn Chase left the room, promising coffee, and a little later a doctor and a gaggle of nurses did things with the paraphernalia that surrounded Spencer. When she whispered sharply, "What's happening?" the doctor said, "It's okay—he's breathing on his own now."

He led her away from the bed. "We don't know yet how much damage the heart has sustained, but we can be hopeful of getting him over this one." He squeezed her arm and left her while he checked on another patient.

Chase came back soon afterward with coffee.

"Why don't you go home?" he suggested when she told him what the doctor said. "Spencer's in good hands and you're bushed. It's been more than twelve hours since he collapsed. I'll stay. Take my car." He paused with the keys in his hand. "If you're all right to drive?"

"Yes. But you've been up as long…"

"I'll snatch a nap later." He took the empty cup from her hand and pressed the keys into her palm. "I promise I'll get hold of you if he needs you."

She slept for several hours, and then drove Chase's car to the *Clarion's* car park and picked up her own, first taking a minute to see Spencer's secretary.

"Chase called," Glenys told her. "He said your father's rallying." Under a layer of makeup she looked as though she'd been crying.

"It must have been a shock for you, finding him like that," Alysia said. At the time she'd been too shocked and worried herself to think about Glenys's feelings, but she remembered now that the secretary had been white-faced and shaking. "You probably saved his life. I'm grateful, Glenys, and I'm sure he is, too."

"Are you…are you going to the hospital now?"

"Yes."

"Would you give him my…my regards, and tell him we're all thinking of him?"

"Of course. He'll appreciate that."

This time Spencer's recovery took longer. "An early retirement might be a good idea," the registrar recommended the day he was moved from intensive care. "It isn't as though you couldn't afford it. Brush up your golf score, grow some roses maybe." The doctor sometimes played golf with Spencer himself. "Persuade him," he urged Alysia.

"Roses," Spencer snorted. He paid a gardener to look after the gardens and lawns. Alysia couldn't imagine him pottering about with secateurs, hunting for caterpillars and black spot.

"You ought to think about what he said, Dad," she said bravely as the doctor left.

Ignoring that, he asked brusquely, "Where's Chase?"

"I expect he's at work." Or getting some sleep. He deserved it, the way he'd been pushing himself lately, holding everything together at the *Clarion.*

"Find a phone and get him here."

"Dad, I don't think the doctors would—"

"Do as you're told, girl. I need to talk to him."

Worrying about the paper and getting angry if she refused to do as he'd ordered wouldn't do his heart any good. She left his bedside and went to find a phone.

After seeing Chase, Spencer fell into an exhausted sleep and Alysia finally went home and lay down, but she soon realized that the insistent throbbing at her temples was going to prevent her from sleeping at all. She went to the bathroom and opened the cupboard, hoping to find some aspirin. The first-aid box yielded only an empty packet.

Her father might have something in his bathroom. She turned and padded along the passageway.

There was a cupboard below the basin. Moving

aside aftershave and male shampoo, a bottle of pre-scription pills with a faded label and a stack of spare toilet rolls, she found a plastic ice-cream container holding a box of Band-Aids, a packet of cough drops and—thank heaven—some paracetamol tablets.

Snatching them up, she bent to replace the con-tainer in the cupboard, and felt it touch something that fell with a glassy thud.

Peering inside the cupboard, she withdrew a small makeup bottle and stared at it in puzzlement. It con-tained liquid foundation, light beige according to the label, and looked quite new.

It certainly wasn't hers, and it couldn't be Mrs. Pearson's. The housekeeper was half Maori and her complexion was definitely not light beige.

There was no way it could have sat here since Aly-sia's mother had died, and in any case it would have been too pale for her, too.

Carefully Alysia replaced the bottle and the plastic container in front of it. She straightened, clutching the painkillers. Her head was fairly thundering now. Stumbling in to the kitchen, she poured a glass of water and took two pills.

Don't think about it, she told herself. This is not the time to think about it.

But her last muzzy thought when the pills took hold and the pain in her head receded enough for her to drift into sleep was that the satin gown in her father's wardrobe had not belonged to her mother.

Alysia spent most of the next few days at the hos-pital. On the third day she told Spencer, "I won't come back tonight. Chase said he'd call after dinner." He brightened then, but soon tired, and she left.

She made herself a light meal and did some washing, then switched on the television and watched a situation comedy and a news backgrounder before Chase knocked on the door.

After leading him into the lounge she switched off the TV set. "How is he tonight?" she asked him.

"Improving, I'd say. If he's sensible I expect he'll be on his feet again soon."

"Do you want coffee or something?"

"I could use a whiskey." He looked tired, too.

"You pour it," she said. "I'll get some ice."

She fetched crushed ice from the freezer in the kitchen, and when he had scooped some into the glass and poured whiskey over it he asked, "Can I fix something for you?"

"A gin and tonic," Alysia decided.

She took a seat on the sofa facing the empty fireplace, and he sat in a chair at right-angles to it, swirling the liquid in his glass before downing it in two gulps only seconds apart.

"More?" Alysia asked.

"No." But he didn't relinquish the glass. The ice cubes in the bottom clinked gently together as he absently moved the glass in tiny circles.

Alysia sipped her drink more slowly. She stared at the brass fan that screened the grate. "Did you know that my father had a mistress?" she asked baldly.

Chase's hand stilled, and there was a dead silence before he said, "I don't believe my employer's love life is any business of mine."

"*Did you know?*"

"Alysia, if your father has a lover—"

"Who is she?"

"Surely it's for him to tell you if he wants to."

"You don't think it's any of *my* business either, do you?" She clutched her glass hard in her hand.

Chase hesitated. "Frankly, no. I suppose it's a bit of a...surprise for you—"

"Yes." She stood up and walked blindly to the window. It was dark outside, and the night was cloudy with few stars.

"How did you find out?"

"It doesn't matter." With her back to him, she said, "You're probably right. It's nothing to do with me."

"Your father is...was...until recently, a fit, vigorous man."

Handsome too, Alysia thought dully, in a mature, intelligent way. She'd seen women smile at him invitingly. It had never crossed her mind that he might have taken any of them up on their tacit invitations. He'd been devoted to her mother. She had always thought that he was faithful to her memory.

Chase said, "How long since your mother died?"

"Eight years."

"Spencer would have been in his early fifties, then," Chase pointed out.

"It's just that I had no idea, and..." And she felt sick at the thought of him taking another woman to the bed he'd shared with her mother.

Immature of her. Even selfish. She ought to be glad that he'd found solace, that he wasn't still grieving as she was. She didn't think the grieving would ever stop. Tonight it had returned in all its painful sharpness.

"You'll get used to the idea," Chase said quietly.

"You know her, don't you?"

Chase waited a moment before he answered. "I believe so, yes."

"Is she...is she much younger than he is?" she asked, dreading the answer.

"I don't think so. Not a lot."

That was a relief. Alysia momentarily closed her eyes. Suddenly hit by an appalling thought, she swung around, finding Chase on his feet. "If she cares for him she'll have been frantic when he got sick! Does she know? Why hasn't she visited him?"

"She has."

Blankly Alysia stared. "You contacted her?" Was this yet another thing that Spencer had shared with Chase, excluding her? The sinister serpent of jealousy that she'd thought banished hissed again within her.

Chase shook his head. "Not exactly."

"I'm there every day. The only woman I know of who's been to visit him is Glenys."

"Yes," Chase said.

"So what makes you think—" Alysia stopped, remembering the secretary's reddened eyelids, and her trembling shock when she'd found her employer after his second heart attack. "His *secretary?*"

Chase obviously debated whether to confirm it, and finally shrugged. "It isn't so surprising, you know."

Of course it wasn't. They saw each other daily, understood each other, no doubt, on a working basis that had easily spilled over into the personal sphere.

"I've been so naive."

How many times when Spencer said he was working late had he actually been visiting his mistress? And he'd been so anxious for Alysia to have a social life of her own. To leave the house instead of keeping him company in the evenings.

Was this why he'd seized so eagerly on her suggestion that she attend journalism school after university?

Had he really been grateful for having her home again? Or secretly dismayed?

Chase said, "They say most people find it difficult to cope with their parents' sexuality. If it's any help, I think I know how you feel."

"I feel *stupid!* Do you know how long they've been...been together?"

Chase shook his head. "I think it was an established thing when I came to work for the *Clarion*. It wasn't long before I heard..."

"So everyone knows about it." Except her.

"You know how towns like this are."

Yes, she did. A long-standing secret like that was bound to leak out eventually.

"Sit down, Alysia," he suggested gently.

She must look as though she needed to. He came over and guided her to the sofa, seating himself beside her, one arm behind her resting on the back but not touching her.

She gulped at the drink he'd made her, still absorbing this new revelation, then said abruptly, "Dad's been advised to take an early retirement."

"I know. He told me."

Of course. He told Chase everything, didn't he? Chase knew more about her father than she did. Alysia drank some more without tasting it. "Did he say he would consider it?"

"He'd be a fool not to."

"The doctor said he should take up growing roses."

"Roses?" Chase's brows shot up.

"Can you imagine it?" Alysia began to laugh.

Chase grinned down at her and, as if obeying an impulse, bent and silenced her laughter with his mouth.

Yes, Alysia's mind said as she met his kiss with her lips parted and eager. This was what she needed tonight, to stop her thinking, stop her hurting. This mindless blotting out of everything but the most primitive emotion of them all—raw, elemental desire.

Her head rested on his encircling arm, and his hand skimmed over the material of her top, pulled it from her jeans and found the bare skin of her waist. He stroked her back and his fingers unhooked her bra. Alysia arched her spine, and he followed the curve of it with his hand until the waistband of her jeans stopped him. He hitched her closer, and as his mouth scorched along her throat, dropping kisses down the taut line of it, she gave a sigh of half regret, half thankfulness.

She snuggled closer, bringing one leg up so that her thigh lay against his hip.

Chase gave a muttered exclamation and said in her ear, "Alysia, do you know what you're doing?"

She turned her head, catching his upper lip between hers, then the lower one, and briefly nipped at them with her teeth. "I think so. I can feel it." Boldly she inserted her hand between them.

He shuddered, and when he spoke his voice was hoarse. "Alysia, *don't!*" He took her wrist, forcing it away from him. "Damn, stop it!"

"Damn you!" she retorted. "Why don't you finish what you started? Are you waiting for permission from my father?"

"It isn't that."

"Then what the hell is it?" Furious and dissatisfied, she pulled her wrist from his hold.

"I'm no Boy Scout. I didn't come prepared. Sorry."

She ought to have thought of that, Alysia realized. Perhaps she should have prepared for the contingency herself.

But she hadn't planned this, either, and anyway she couldn't imagine going to one of the town's two pharmacies and asking for what they needed. She dropped her head against his shoulder, wondering if she would have gone ahead blindly if he hadn't called a halt.

Chase was kissing the shallow groove just below her ear. "You're a beautiful, passionate woman, and I want you like hell. But on the whole I think I'd rather wait and do this properly."

"Is that a promise?" Alysia demanded.

His laughter was strained. "You bet." He eased himself regretfully away from her and stood up, ran a hand through his hair, then shook his head and picked up his whiskey glass. "D'you mind if I make myself another one of these? It'll be the last. I have to drive."

In other words he wasn't staying. "Be my guest." When he turned around again she was smoothing her hands over her tumbled hair. She picked up her drink.

Chase walked to the window and stood there as she had stood earlier, lifting the glass to his lips.

Alysia finished her gin and tonic and sat cradling the empty glass. She felt empty herself as the hot, rampant desire slowly left her. Leaning her head back against the sofa, she looked almost dispassionately at Chase's rigid back.

Studying his long legs, the taut haunches and nar-

row waist, the broad shoulders and the tilt of his dark
head, she wondered why this particular man could
almost send her over the edge with a touch.

She hadn't even liked him for ages, was sometimes
unsure if she did now. But there was no denying that
something in him called to something in her.

The sexual component was so strong that she was
wary of its power. But there were other things, too.
His obvious intelligence, his occasional humor, the
rare flashes of sensibility and compassion that he'd
shown her. And his rocklike support when her father
was ill, which had crumbled all her defenses and
made her almost alarmingly dependent on him.

Even the self-control and consideration that had
stopped him from taking advantage of her reckless
mood. All the things that made her...love him.

Her head buzzed. She'd admitted it. She was head
over heels in love and she didn't know how he felt
about her.

She wondered tiredly if he'd deliberately neglected
to be prepared because he'd needed the excuse.
Maybe in his way Chase was as wary as she was, if
for different reasons.

She saw his shoulders lift and sag, and he turned
to face her, as if he'd felt her scrutiny. "Are you all
right?" he asked her.

"Yes." She supposed she ought to be ashamed of
her behavior. Maybe she would be later. Right now
she felt too drained for any other emotion to intrude.
Even the confused tension that so often pervaded her
meetings with Chase was mercifully absent.

"Maybe it isn't the right time for this, either,"
Chase said, as if making up his mind about something, "but I need to know... Alysia, will you marry
me?"

Chapter Nine

At first she could only stare at him.

"Did you hear me?" he prompted her. "I just proposed to you, Alysia."

In the back of her mind, she realized, there had been a core of conviction that Chase would resist the pressures of her father's obvious wishes and his own ambition. She knew he wanted her physically, but he had never said he loved her, and she couldn't help noticing the glaring omission even now.

"I heard you," she said. Bewilderingly, her chief emotion was a tearing disappointment.

At least he hadn't lied. Chase was basically honest. He'd never made any secret of his determination to climb to the top, and he wasn't fussy about the means he used. If he couldn't let Spencer down, he'd take whatever sweetener was offered.

But she wanted more from him—she wanted his love, she realized with dismay and more pain than she'd ever imagined possible.

The sex promised to be great, she admitted bleakly, forcing herself to pragmatism. And maybe when the novelty of that wore off they'd have found some other, firmer foundation on which to build a lasting marriage. Maybe Chase might learn to love her...as her father had.

Her father would be pleased. He was fond of her but he'd never really needed her, even when he was ill. She'd just been getting in the way, preventing him from enjoying the support and help of a woman who had been devoted to him for years.

"If you need to think about it..." Chase offered, his frowning gaze on her face.

"No," she said thinly. "I mean, yes." Why not? She was used to half loaves, and wasn't that supposed to be better than none? Maybe in time Chase would love her for herself. She'd lived most of her life on hope and illusion. This time there was no illusion. She knew what she was being offered, less than she wanted but perhaps all she could expect. Her chin lifting, she said clearly, "Yes, I'll marry you."

Chase slowly walked toward her. "Thank you," he said, and then smiled, taking her hands. "You've made me a very happy man."

There, she said to herself. It was that easy. "I'm happy, too," she said politely. Curiously, she felt totally emotionless.

Chase gave a short, puzzled laugh and pulled her to her feet, linking his arms loosely about her waist. "Are you?" His eyes searched her face. "You won't change your mind?"

Alysia shook her head. "I won't change my mind." The chill that seemed to have descended on her soul began to recede. *I want you like hell,* he'd told her fifteen minutes ago. Well, she wanted him too, and now she was getting him. She should be ecstatic.

He lifted her chin and kissed her very gently, like a solemn promise. "I was forgetting how tired you must be," he told her. "I'll go, and let you get to bed." He tucked his arm about her and took her with him to the door. There he kissed her again lightly, on the cheek this time.

"Good night," he said. "You needn't come back to work, you know. We'll manage without you."

She smiled wanly at that. Nobody really needed her. No one in the whole wide world.

Spencer received the news without surprise. As far as he was concerned it had been foreordained from the time he'd decided that pairing his daughter and his deputy editor was a good idea. She could almost see him congratulating himself on the success of his plans.

After he came home Alysia continued to look after his needs, and this time he didn't try to go back to work, making only token appearances in the office.

Chase bought her a ring, a classic diamond solitaire, and Spencer announced their engagement in the *Clarion*, with a photograph taken by a staff photographer to accompany the short paragraph about Chase's career and the Kingsley family's historic connections with both the paper and the town.

Perfect strangers stopped Alysia in the street offering their good wishes. The staff of the *Clarion* sent her a card, and Glenys came to the house with a bouquet for her and a homemade cake. "The recipe is approved by the Heart Foundation,'' she assured Alysia.

"It's very kind of you,'' Alysia said. "Come in. I'm sure my father would like to talk to you.''

She went off to brew tea, taking her time. When she entered the lounge Glenys was sitting primly on a chair opposite her father's while they talked about office affairs.

Alysia made an excuse to leave, closing the door behind her. But when she heard the voices cease and the lounge door open she hurried to the passageway.

"I'm just leaving,'' Glenys said. "I told your father not to get up.'' As Alysia escorted her to the door, she said, "He seems older. Not himself at all.''

"I'm sure your visit will have done him good,'' Alysia said. "Please come by anytime. I know you're very close to him.''

The woman cast her a startled glance and flushed. "I don't want to intrude...''

"Please,'' Alysia said firmly, "never think you're intruding. My father must have missed you very much.''

Glenys looked down at the bag she clutched tightly in two hands, then sent a searching, embarrassed look at Alysia. "Oh, well...well, thank you. I...perhaps I will call in sometimes.''

Alysia's faint hope of a quiet, low-key wedding was quickly dashed. Spencer was determined that this was going to be an occasion the town would remember. He planned a lavish affair involving an army of caterers, photographers, musicians, florists and organizers, plus a couturier gown, a fleet of wedding cars, and the hiring and decorating of the biggest public lounge in town.

Chase kissed her every time they saw each other, but he seldom went further than kisses, his lovemaking more circumspect than it had ever been.

Maybe, she thought with gloomy cynicism, the excitement and desire had lessened for him now that he was certain of his eventual conquest. She couldn't help thinking of it as ownership, although Chase had said that he wouldn't ask her to promise obedience. And he'd laughed when she'd fixed him with a level look and said, "Just as well, because I wouldn't."

Sandra, also sporting a new engagement ring from Hurley, suggested, "We should do a foursome one night. There's a nightclub just starting up. Why don't we catch the opening?"

When Alysia passed on the invitation to Chase he said, "Good idea. We did a feature on the club, so I have free tickets for the opening night anyway."

"Maybe Glenys might like to keep you company," she told Spencer. "We could be late coming home."

"I don't need a nursemaid," Spencer snapped. "I wish you'd stop asking that woman around here."

Alysia looked at him in surprise. "I thought you...liked her."

"I didn't say I don't like her. I just don't want her to get...mistaken ideas."

"Mistaken?"

"I've never wanted to replace your mother, Alysia."

Alysia decided to stop beating about the bush. "I understood that you and Glenys were rather more than friends."

"Who told you that?" Color suffusing his face,

Spencer cleared his throat and muttered, "Well, you're not a child anymore."

"No, I'm not. And if you've been making yourself and Glenys unhappy on my account, I wish you'd stop."

"It's nothing to do with you! I admit I was reluctant to...to make public my personal relationship with my secretary, the fact that I had a young daughter being one reason. But it...the, er, relationship no longer exists."

Alysia was puzzled. "She's very fond of you."

Spencer gave a bark of bitter laughter. "It was a convenient arrangement that suited us both, but since my illness I haven't been able to fulfill a woman's needs. Is that plain enough for you?" He glared.

Alysia thought of Glenys's inadequately disguised anguish after she'd found him ill, and a flash of anger hit her. "That woman is *devoted* to you," she said fiercely. "How can you reduce your relationship with her to a *convenient arrangement?* You must have some feelings for her!"

Spencer was plainly taken aback. "My feelings are none of your business, miss!"

Swallowing her indignation, Alysia said, "Have you discussed your...the problem with her?"

"Certainly not!"

"I've read a lot about heart disease lately," she said quietly. "It's probably a temporary thing. What did the doctor say?"

"I didn't mention it."

He'd been too embarrassed, she guessed, to discuss it with his erstwhile golf partner. "Why don't you talk to Glenys? She seems to me like a sensible, compassionate woman."

"I'm not interested in any woman's compassion!" Spencer burst out. "This is not a conversation I find suitable to have with my daughter!" And he stalked out of the room.

Alysia left Spencer on his own while she went nightclubbing, so she insisted that it mustn't be too late when Chase took her home.

"When am I going to meet your mother?" she asked him as the car started up the hill toward the house.

Chase looked at her for a second, then returned his attention to the road. "Do you want to?"

"Of course I want to." Presumably his mother would be at the wedding, but wasn't it usual to meet one's fiancé's parents before that? "Where does she live?"

"On the Gold Coast now."

"Australia?"

"Yes. Her husband owns property there."

"What kind of property?"

"Apartment buildings, business premises."

So his stepfather had money, probably a good deal of money. "Did my father ask you about him?"

"What do you think?"

Of course he had asked, if not when Chase took the job of reporter on the *Clarion*, then later, when Spencer began to think that his protege might make a suitable husband for his daughter.

And what does your father do, young man?

My stepfather is a property developer in Queensland, sir. Conjuring up pictures of luxury high-rise apartments and houses worth millions of dollars. The Gold Coast wasn't called that for nothing.

It wouldn't even occur to Spencer to ask about Chase's mother. In his view women didn't do anything that mattered, especially if their husbands had money.

Alysia began to laugh.

"What's funny?" Chase pressed his foot on the accelerator and the car speeded up the hill.

She couldn't tell him. "Nothing, really."

He turned in to the driveway, slowing to a whispering halt in front of the door. Then he swung around and hauled her into his arms, stopping the lingering laughter and covering her mouth in an all-consuming kiss. She could hardly breathe, and when she made a protesting movement his mouth hardened on hers, pushing her head back against the seat.

Alysia closed her teeth on his lower lip.

He made a low exclamation and let her go.

Breathless and a little nervous, Alysia said, "I wasn't laughing at you. You're still oversensitive."

"I guess." He touched a finger to his lip. "Sorry. I've never done that to a woman before."

"Am I supposed to be thrilled?"

His eyes lifted, flaring in the dim light. "No, *I'm* supposed to be ashamed. I am."

She hadn't broken the skin, but she felt slightly guilty. "Does it hurt?" she asked.

"I think I'll live."

She should open the door, leave him to drive home reflecting on his sins. Instead she inched slowly across the seat toward him.

Chase didn't react, and she lifted her mouth to touch his abused lower lip, just a bare touch, light as a butterfly's wing. She withdrew no more than an inch, then did it again, and again.

Chase remained perfectly still, one arm along the back of the seat, the other resting on the rim of the steering wheel, his back rigid.

She took his lip between hers, very gently, and ran the tip of her tongue over the throbbing, hot place where she'd bitten him. Then she drew away again, looking at his mouth. The lower lip was fuller than usual, moist and glistening. "Better?" she whispered.

"I could do with some more...treatment," he suggested.

Alysia leaned closer, until her breasts pressed against his chest. She felt him take a quick breath but he still didn't move.

There was something deliciously exciting about trying to seduce this silent, seemingly unresponsive man. She gave him another soft, tantalizing kiss, this time on both lips, then raised her hand and ran her fingertip lightly over the swollen lower one.

His arms came around her like a vise, bending her backward as he accepted her kiss eagerly, giving her the passion she craved. She hooked her own arms around his neck, her breasts straining against his chest, reveling in the hard warmth of him.

When they surfaced she touched his mouth again with her thumb. "Isn't it sore?"

"Yes," he said. "But I must have a latent masochistic streak." And he kissed her again.

Twenty minutes later he saw her into the house, and she entered with her legs shaking, her whole body suffused with unslaked need.

Languorously she made her way up the stairs to her room and undressed, pulling on a thin white robe. In the bathroom the light seemed overbright, making her blink.

She paused before the mirror, struck by a view of herself she'd never seen before. Her cheeks were delicately flushed, her eyes lustrous and emerald-green, her mouth devoid of lipstick but red and full like rose petals. And her hair tumbled around her face, shadowing her cheekbones and giving her an air of mysterious beauty. Was this how Chase saw her?

A strange emotion took hold of her; her head lifted proudly, and she felt her heart beat faster. In the mirror she saw how her breasts were outlined under the clinging gown, the centers still peaked and prominent, shadowy dark against the white material. She would look like this on her wedding night.

Excitement thickened her throat, and she cupped her hands under her breasts, remembering, and anticipating Chase's hands there.

She breathed in deeply. The wedding was less than a month away. Time she was thinking about a trousseau. Sexy underwear and lingerie, the traditional trappings of a bride. Lots of satin and lace, old-fashioned nightgowns with long skirts, slits and minimal bodices, tiny panties and half-cup bras, sheer stockings, maybe a garter belt or two, thongs—red, black?

She'd have him on his knees.

Spencer assumed that Alysia and Chase would make their home with him after their marriage. And what other choice was there? With an unsound heart, Spencer couldn't be left on his own.

Builders were called in to convert two bedrooms into a larger bedroom-cum-sitting room with its own bathroom, and glass doors opening onto a private balcony. The architect Spencer hired incorporated the alterations without spoiling the integrity of the building.

"You choose how you want it redecorated," Spencer told Alysia. "This is my wedding present to you and Chase."

So the big room had been hung with a pale green and silver wallpaper and the woodwork painted white.

With Chase's approval Alysia took a brass-ended double bed from one of the other rooms and had it resprung and fitted with a new, comfortable mattress. She'd bought pale green sheets, had a duvet cover made to match the pattern of small leaves on the curtains, and added a couple of antique kauri dressers and a chaise newly upholstered in green and softened with cushions.

She hung her clothes on one side of the walk-in wardrobe, and the day before the wedding Chase brought a couple of suitcases over and installed his clothes on the other side.

He was staying for dinner, and his mother and stepfather, who had flown over from Australia and were booked into the town's best hotel, had been invited.

Spencer's sister was spending the night at the house, but Valda and her husband had refused an offer to do the same. "The kids would be too much for Spencer," Valda said. "We'll find a motel, and I'll be there first thing in the morning to help you get ready."

Alysia's bridesmaids were Sandra and a university friend, with Valda's small daughter as flower girl.

Chase went to get his parents, and when she heard the car arrive Alysia opened the front door.

Rita Osborne was taller than Alysia, her figure comfortably rounded. She had dark brown, softly waved hair greying in front, and her hazel eyes were warm but anxious. She kissed Alysia's cheek a little awkwardly and said, "I am *so* pleased to meet you, Alysia."

"I'm happy to meet you, too," Alysia responded. "I hope we're going to be friends." She turned to shake hands with the tall, spare man beside Rita.

Graeme Osborne smiled at her and said, "My stepson is a lucky man."

Just how lucky he discovered after dinner, when Alysia and her aunt had cleared the table and they were all in the lounge with their coffee.

Spencer put down his cup and cleared his throat. "I have made certain arrangements in regard to this marriage and my daughter's future. As this affects your son too—" he looked at Graeme and Rita Osborne "—I think you're entitled to hear it."

Alysia felt her stomach churn. What was Spencer planning?

She soon found out.

"This is an appropriate time to announce that I have decided to hand over my responsibilities at the *Clarion*." He cleared his throat. "As of next week Chase will become editor-in-chief of the newspaper, and chief executive of the business."

The titles that had always been reserved for family.

Graeme turned to his stepson. "Congratulations."

His mother smiled and held out her hand to him. "I'm so proud of you, son!"

He smiled back at her and then looked at Spencer. "Thank you for your confidence in me, sir."

"I know the newspaper will be in good hands. And, so that the business remains in the family," Spencer said, "I've established a trust, of which both

Alysia and Chase and any of their children will be the beneficiaries. The newspaper remains in his hands so long as he is married to Alysia. On my death Alysia will be the sole beneficiary of the income from other Kingsley family properties and stocks and shares, while the newspaper becomes her and Chase's joint property, along with this house, devolving to their children in due course."

Patricia was looking confused but approving, and Chase's parents vaguely pleased. It was obvious none of them understood exactly what it all meant.

They probably thought that while Chase was getting a promotion, Alysia was doing very well out of the deal, with a lifetime income and joint ownership of the *Clarion*. It sounded fine, an insurance against Chase gaining any of her family's assets if their marriage didn't last. But she knew what it really meant— a token share for her, real power for Chase. Because Chase was the one Spencer had put firmly into his own place.

Someone had circled her head with a heavy iron band and turned the screws. She seemed to be the only one who was aware that her father had stripped away her inheritance and robbed her of her identity.

The newspaper belonged to the Kingsleys, as the Kingsleys belonged to the town. Spencer Kingsley had given his name to her, but he had taken away the symbol of her membership in the family and handed it over to an outsider. To Chase. Even her children would only inherit if they were also his.

She felt Chase's eyes on her, and sat in frozen silence, unable to look at him, unwilling to see the triumph in his eyes.

Her stomach churned sickly. This was what he had

wanted all along, and he'd found the only way to get it.

What a fool she'd been. A blind, easily manipulated fool.

Her hands trembled on her coffee cup. She wanted to throw it across the room, to stand up and scream her frustration and rage and hurt.

Instead she put down the cup, stood up and said quite calmly, "If nobody minds, I think I'll go to bed."

"Yes, dear. Your big day tomorrow," Patricia said. "You're looking a bit washed-out. Wedding preparations are tiring. Have a good sleep, and tomorrow you'll be a radiant bride."

"It's been lovely to meet you at last." Her smile skimmed over Graeme and Rita.

Rita smiled back at her. "We should be going soon. It's been a long day for us, too."

Alysia was halfway up the stairs when she heard Chase bounding up behind her. She tried to hurry on but he caught her arm and went past her, barring her way. "Are you all right?" he asked, his eyes darkened.

Her own eyes burned. She said with false, high-pitched gaiety, "Yes, of course. What could possibly be wrong? Tomorrow's my wedding day. Yours too. The day my father gets all he ever wanted."

Chase frowned. "Alysia—?"

But now the others came in to the hall, talking, and Patricia was at the bottom of the stairs. "Your parents are ready to go back to the motel, Chase. Your mother's tired after their journey."

"Yes, coming," Chase said, and looked searchingly at Alysia. "Darling—"

"They're waiting for you." She continued her climb up the stairs, but he shot out a hand and detained her. She wouldn't look at him.

"I love you," he said rapidly, intensely. "Don't forget that." He bent and kissed her, swift and fierce. "Be there tomorrow."

Did he think she wouldn't be?

She hoped the possibility would keep him awake tonight.

Chapter Ten

After endless staring into the darkness and trying not to think, Alysia was scarcely five minutes late for the ceremony. When her father said, "Are you ready?" she numbly took his arm and walked slowly down the aisle to the strains of the wedding march.

This is what you want, she told herself. What we all want. No matter that Chase might not have been so eager to marry her without the dowry that her father had so generously offered him.

And anyway, would her father ever forgive her for leaving Chase at the altar? Making both men look like fools before all the friends and relatives and important citizens that Spencer had proudly invited to the wedding of his daughter and his protege?

Refusing to go through with this would be one sure way of losing literally everything she held dear. Chase, her father's precarious love and any last lingering claim on the inheritance she'd taken for granted all her life. Even her home. In the unlikely event that Spencer didn't wash his hands of her, she'd never be able to stay in Waikura after causing such a scandal.

She'd gamble on making Chase love her, in time. Because the alternative was losing him. And that would be infinitely worse than losing the *Clarion,* than losing her heritage. Strange what love could do to a person. Everything she'd taken for granted, looked forward to all her life, paled beside her crying need for this one, flawed man.

She was going through with this, no matter what it cost her. There was no other choice except that dictated by a mad urge to smash this whole castle of dreams in a dramatic, last-minute fit of childish rage.

The church aisle seemed very long, the altar and the robed minister before it far, far away.

Her dress was classic white silk and lace with a veil that made her vision misty. Maybe that was why Chase looked impossibly handsome as he waited for her, his face serious and expectant and tense.

Alysia looked away from him to the altar, decorated with great bowls of professionally arranged white and gold flowers. Then at last she was standing beside him and her knees started to tremble.

She gave her responses as if she were performing in a play, her voice low but firm. The first jolt of reality intruded when Chase placed his ring on her finger. His palm was warm under hers, his fingers strong but not quite steady, and she looked up. His expression was grave and granitelike, but his gaze was fixed on their hands.

Then it was over, and he lifted the veil from her face and bent to kiss her, a mere brushing of his mouth over hers that she scarcely felt and couldn't return. She might have been a marble statue.

Alysia signed the register with fingers that shook, and placed her hand on her husband's arm for the long walk back down the aisle.

She smiled for the cameras until her jaw ached, and accepted kisses, handshakes and congratulations, and at the reception sat at the bridal table while speeches were made and smiled some more.

There was dancing, and when the music started Chase held out his arms and Alysia went into them. She was feeling very floaty, because she had eaten only a little of what was the finest food available from the most expensive caterers in Waikura, but had drunk a considerable quantity of sparkling wine. She had taken off her veil and had to hold up the train of her dress.

Everything seemed unreal. It had been that way since her father's announcement last night, as if she weren't actually here but was outside the scene, watching herself with slightly contemptuous eyes from afar.

She danced with her father and Howard and some others and then Chase reclaimed her. He held her in his arms and they swayed to the music together, and after a while he whispered, "Would you like to slip off now?"

She just stopped herself from replying with an indifferent shrug. That wasn't the way a bride was supposed to act, and she'd put her all into acting the bride today, for the sake of her pride and her father's peace of mind. She nodded. "If you like."

They had plane tickets booked for Australia the following day but tonight they were returning to the house while Spencer spent the night with the Franklins.

Chase danced them nearer to the door, grasped her hand and said, "Come on. We'll make a run for it."

The best man had given Chase the keys of his car, and they almost made it before a laughing group caught up and began showering them with confetti.

Chase chose a roundabout route in case they were followed, but eventually drew up outside the house.

"Did Dad give you a key?" she asked.

He took it from his pocket, got out of the car and started brushing confetti off his suit.

Alysia climbed out without waiting and shook some of the stuff from the folds of her dress.

"Wait a minute." Bounding up the steps, he unlocked the door and threw it wide, switched on the light, and then came back and swung her into his arms.

Gazing down at her, he said, "You looked very lovely today. Did I tell you?"

He hadn't, but she'd seen it in his eyes every time he looked at her. He might not love her, despite his desperate, belated declaration last night, when he must have guessed that she might be tempted to go back on her promise to marry him, but he wanted her in a physical sense. And in a purely practical one as well. She had that to hold on to. And to help her hold him. "Tell me again," she demanded.

"You are a gorgeous, sexy woman," he said. "And I've been waiting forever to make love to you." He started climbing the steps. "Which I hope to do every night for the rest of our lives."

Inside he slammed the door shut with his foot, and continued up the stairs and along the passageway to their newly decorated room. She had left a bedside lamp on, and it cast a soft glow among the shadows.

He seated her on the bed and said, "Do you want the bathroom first?"

"You can have it if you like. I have to get out of this dress."

"No way," he said. "My job. I've been fantasizing about it ever since I saw you coming down the aisle."

"In church?"

"With my body I thee worship." He stripped off his jacket and tugged at his tie. "I won't be long."

And with all my worldly goods I thee endow. Only the line was supposed to be his.

Stop that. As he closed the door behind him Alysia kicked off her shoes and took them to the wardrobe. She pulled out a new satin robe, long, silver and perfectly plain, with a tie belt.

The garment's cool, simple elegance had stood out among the lace and frills in the lingerie shop. When she'd tried it on and looked in the shop mirror she'd suddenly seemed taller and slimmer, and very glamorous. And the color made her eyes go a mysterious silver-green.

She hung it over the brass bed end, and stripped off the covers. She was turning down the sheets when the bathroom door opened and Chase emerged, his shirt open and the sleeves unbuttoned, his belt and the fastening at the top of his pants undone. His hair was damp in front and he'd shaved again.

He looked so handsome and sexy she felt a hot melting sensation that started in her throat and traveled rapidly all the way to her toes.

He came over to her and said, "Just let me look at you for a minute."

He did, thoroughly, from the pinned-up hairstyle that had held the regal pearl headdress securing her veil, down past the round neckline of her gown to the way it fitted over her breasts and defined her waist, and flared into fullness over her hips. "My princess bride," he murmured.

He reached out and skimmed his hands from her shoulders down her arms to her wrists. Lifting her hands, he took the very tips of her fingers one by one into his mouth, nibbling on them with his lips.

He released her fingers and clasped her waist, drawing her towards him, and kissed her forehead, her nose, her cheeks, his lips softly progressing down to the curve of her shoulder, and the hollow of her throat. He touched her breasts, and eased her forward to fit her lower body against him before he found her mouth with his in a long, seductive kiss. Slow heat flowed through her, a delicious trickle of desire.

Maybe she could forget, for this one night, why he had married her. If she let her body take over, blanked out her mind.

His hands wandered up her back to the row of tiny buttons fastening her dress, and he drew back his head and loosened his hold, saying, "Turn around."

Alysia obeyed, and as he flipped open the first button she felt his lips teasing her nape. She closed her eyes, concentrating on the sensation that evoked. *Don't think.*

Another button followed, and his mouth moved an inch lower. By the time he reached the last button at the base of her spine his mouth had almost caught up with his fingers.

The dress fell to the floor, a gleaming white pool around her feet, revealing a satin and lace bra, and matching French panties over a garter belt and sheer silk stockings. And Chase was kneeling on the carpet. She looked down at his dark head and her throat ached.

His hands circled her thighs in the gap between the stockings and the panties and she felt him press another kiss there, and then he undid the clips that held the stockings and smoothed the filmy nylon down her legs, lifting her feet one by one to pull the stockings right off. His dark hair brushed against her thigh.

She'd promised herself she'd have him on his knees. But he didn't seem like a supplicant.

He stood up, gliding his hands the length of her legs, over her hips to her waist, and turned her to him again, looking down at her breasts rising from the lace cups of the bra, before he raised his gaze to her face. "If I'm dreaming," he said, "don't wake me up."

Alysia stepped back, careful of the expensive satin pooled about her feet. "Bathroom," she said, and bent to pick up the dress.

"I'll fix this," Chase told her, taking it from her. "Hurry back."

Taking the silver robe, she showered, brushed her teeth, applied a smidgeon of shadow to her eyelids, a hint of color to her lips, and sprayed herself with an expensive, subtle floral perfume.

Before returning to the bedroom she pulled on the robe and loosely fastened the belt. Her wedding dress and stockings were gone from the floor and Chase lounged on the bed wearing grape-colored pajama pants, one foot on the sheepskin rug by the bed, the other across his knee, a hand grasping his ankle.

"That's nice." His gaze was on the silver satin.

"Thank you." Alysia went to the dresser with the mirror and started pulling pins from her hair.

Chase's reflection appeared behind hers. Without a word he began to help, and in the end she dropped her hands and let him finish the task. He was so gentle, she could almost pretend this was love. But he'd always known how to be gentle with a woman. She wasn't the first for him.

She would make damned sure she was the last. That was one thing her father had done for her. If Chase strayed he would lose everything.

He put the last pin down and fanned the soft fine strands about her shoulders. She leaned back, and his hands slipped over the satin to rest on the swell of her breasts. Alysia murmured approval and moved against him, her eyelids drifting down.

Chase found the loose knot of her belt and unfastened it. Then he turned her around, parting the robe so that her naked breasts came into contact with his chest.

Alysia gasped. Chase's hands swept down her back to bring her still closer.

She lifted her face and sought his mouth, and he gave it in a seeking, searing kiss. He picked her up in his arms again without shifting his mouth from hers, and carried her to the bed, sinking down on it.

Her hands roved to the smooth warm skin of his back, over the angles of his shoulder blades, buried themselves in his hair. He drew away from her mouth and began kissing her body, worshipping her with his lips and his hands. And she reciprocated with little, searching kisses of her own.

When she was almost afraid she was going to burst

into flame, he nudged her thighs apart. "You have done this before?" he asked hoarsely.

Alysia couldn't speak. She shook her head, her hair tumbled on the pillow.

Chase made a low exclamation and hesitated.

She grabbed his shoulders, her fingers digging in to his flesh.

Chase's jaw was rigidly clenched. She saw him swallow. "I'll be as careful as I can, darling."

It was at first strange, this warm, hard intrusion into her body. Then it was excruciating and she bit her lip, her eyes flying wide.

"I'll stop," he said, and she felt his whole body clench with the effort.

"I don't want you to stop."

He groaned. "I'm hurting you."

He was, but the pain was mixed with the white-heat of desire that had dimmed but not totally receded, and with a driving need to reach the peak of this mysterious, unfamiliar experience. "I want..."

She didn't know what she wanted. Oh, she knew what to call it, but this wasn't like anything she'd read or heard about, this craving for a fulfillment that she knew he could bring her to. "Maybe," she gasped, "you're not the only closet masochist around."

Chase laughed in a breathless, pained way, and bent to kiss her mouth, a careful coaxing with his lips and tongue. "Better?" he asked her.

"A bit." The strange, stretched feeling was bearable now.

He inched closer to the goal, and she breathed deeply and tried to accommodate him, to relax and allow it to happen. "Don't stop," she whispered.

"All right." He kissed her again, and moved a little, and a little more. "God knows," he said, "I don't want to hurt you, Princess, but I have to tell you this is great for me."

A tiny ripple of pleasant sensation began from where he filled her and it radiated outward, followed by another and another, each stronger than the last. She drew her legs up and dug her teeth into her lip, and Chase said anxiously, "It's too painful for you."

"No!" she said, frantically shaking her head as the ripples grew into a tide. "No..." The word turned into a luxurious, sighing moan. Wave after wave of sensation washed over her, and she closed her eyes and let it take her, lift her, toss her over the crest.

She heard him say, "Alysia?" And then, "My God, Princess!"

She hadn't thought it was possible for him to go any deeper but he did, and as she began to float on the other side of the waves Chase's determined restraint finally shattered; his arms gripped her desperately close, his body convulsed against her, he threw back his head with a primal cry of satisfaction, and she knew, triumphantly, that he too was taken by the irresistible force and thrown in the same dizzying maelstrom.

A few minutes later Chase put his lips to her cheek. "Are you okay?"

"Yes." It had been worth it, she thought. For this. To have Chase lose himself in her so fully, so completely, that she could at least pretend for a little while that he loved her.

If it hadn't been exactly perfect for her, it had still been better than she'd realistically thought a first time would be.

"You're so brave," he said, a kind of anguish in his eyes. "Did it hurt badly?"

"For a short while. It's all right."

He kissed her mouth very softly, without passion. "Now?"

"A bit sore," she admitted, but when he made to withdraw she said, "Don't move. I want you to stay."

He eased himself up so that he wasn't so heavy, and kissed her again. "I should have asked sooner. If I'd known I would have waited, taken things slowly. There are other things we could have done tonight. It didn't have to be all at once."

"It's my wedding night. I didn't want half measures. Besides," she added, "there's probably a proviso in that trust deed that says you don't get the *Clarion* until the marriage is consummated. I wouldn't have been surprised if my father had demanded to see a bloodied sheet."

She felt his arms go rigid, his shoulders stiffen. *"What?"* He stared at her.

"It doesn't matter." She shifted her gaze from his and ran a hand down his chest, skimming her nails over his skin. "Forget I said it." She touched a fingertip to one of his nipples, traced the tiny circle and said, "This is cute."

"Alysia!"

Her other hand came over his mouth, and she lifted one of her legs, rubbing her thigh against him. Her foot hooked between his legs, stroking. "Later," she said, "you can show me some of those things we might have done instead."

He moved her hand from his mouth. "Alysia—"

She stopped playing with his nipple and pulled his head down to kiss him, her mouth parted, her tongue gliding along the roof of his mouth. She moved her hips in implicit invitation and felt his instant response as she tightened about him. He groaned against her mouth, slid a hand under her, cupping her flesh, bringing her closer, going deeper still.

This time it was even better. Very nearly perfect.

Alysia woke to the sound of the shower running in the bathroom. She saw the indentation in the pillow next to hers, and felt the warm place on the sheet beside her. The clock on the bedside table said it was nearly eight. They had to leave before midday to catch their flight to Sydney.

She rolled over, threw back the covers and found her robe on the floor.

As she fastened the belt she saw the stain on the sheet, and her fingers stilled for a moment before she pulled the knot tight. After stripping the bed, she ran downstairs to the laundry, thrusting the sheets into the washing machine. When Chase walked out of the bathroom with a towel round his waist she was making up the bed again.

"I thought I heard you moving about." He was rubbing his damp hair with another towel, but he stopped and watched her.

When she straightened and headed for the bathroom, he caught her waist as she passed him. "You okay?"

"Very. Thank you." Last night she'd drifted into sleep still held in his arms, so exhausted that she thought she'd never wake again, let alone that his merest touch would set her singingly alive, every nerve ending alert and expectant.

"Last night—" He looked, for once, slightly un-

"It was great," she said, giving him a wide and not insincere smile.

"You said something—" he went on doggedly.

"I need the bathroom," she interrupted, slipping away from his light hold. "And we'd better get a move on, hadn't we, if we're not going to miss the plane?" She hurried in to the other room and closed the door. The air was a little steamy despite the automatic fan, and it smelled faintly and pleasantly of male cologne.

They were married, for better or for worse. She'd gone in to this with her eyes open, determined to make the best of it.

So keep your mouth shut and get on with it. She turned the shower on full and discarded the robe.

It had been a wonderful wedding night. Chase had been tender and passionate and considerate, and she was a very lucky woman. Lots of people never got what they really wanted out of life, and not many of them had reasonable looks, a big house to live in, a ruggedly attractive, successful husband who was also an incredibly good lover and plenty of money.

Wanting any more than that was just greedy. Stepping under the shower, Alysia lifted her face to let the warm water run over it. She took a bottle of shampoo from the shelf and lathered some into her hair.

But it wasn't the shampoo that made her eyes sting with tears.

Chapter Eleven

They spent two nights in a Sydney hotel and attended a concert at the Opera House. Alysia could hardly concentrate on the music, she was so intensely aware of Chase's long, strong fingers wrapped around hers, the back of her hand resting on the taut muscles of his thigh.

Then they flew north to enjoy sun, sand and scenery, taking a day trip to explore the spectacular corals and sea life of the Great Barrier Reef. And at night they locked themselves into their hotel room and explored each other.

Driving south from there they visited a pineapple plantation. They bought one of the prickly fruit and attacked it that evening in their hotel room with an inadequate knife and ended up covered in sweet-sour sticky juice.

"We need to eat this in the shower," Alysia complained, a piece of the fruit dripping juice all the way down her arm.

"Good idea," Chase agreed instantly. Picking up the plate, he led her to the bathroom and, over her laughing protests, undressed her and himself and bundled her into the dry shower stall, where he fed her pieces of pineapple until she shook her head, saying, "I can't eat any more."

Chase put the plate on the floor outside and turned on the water mixer.

The warm water cascaded over them both, and while she laughed and wriggled in his grasp, he kissed her, tasting of pineapple.

"You're crazy!" Alysia gasped as he raised his head and adjusted the flow so that the water hit his shoulders. But the words sounded unconvincing, and when he kissed her again and she felt him surge against her she flung her wet arms around his neck.

Within minutes they were out of the shower and on the big bed in the other room.

Chase called his mother at Alysia's urging and she invited them to stay overnight.

"Let's do that," Alysia said.

Chase looked surprised. "If you like."

His mother and stepfather lived in an apartment commanding magnificent views of the sea. They had dinner in front of open doors leading onto a narrow balcony while the setting sun spread a warm pink wash over the water all the way to the horizon. Afterward Graeme suggested a walk on the beach.

As they strolled along the broad, firm expanse of sand, with the waves smoothing out the footmarks of the day, Alysia found herself alongside her mother-in-law while the two men strode ahead.

"It looks like a nice place to live," Alysia said.

"We love it. I felt guilty about leaving Charl...Chase behind in New Zealand. He was only twenty, but he wanted to get ahead on his own, make his mark."

Rita stopped, then went on almost defiantly, "He told you, didn't he? When I said I wouldn't come to the wedding he said...he'd told you about me and you wanted to meet me anyway."

"He told me...a bit."

"I ran away from home when I was fifteen. We lived in a mill town. My father was a bully and my mother was too scared of him to stand up for any of us kids. I went to Auckland looking for work. There wasn't much available for fifteen-year-old girls with no skills or qualifications. So I ended up on the streets." Rita cast her a sideways glance.

Alysia wasn't shocked, but she felt a pang of angry sympathy.

"It didn't last long," Rita went on philosophically, "but long enough for me to get pregnant."

Alysia tried to imagine how that must have been for a fifteen-year-old, alone and with no one to care for her. She shook her head to dispel the picture.

"Everyone said get rid of it, but I didn't want to. For the first time in my life I had something to live for, someone to love."

Alysia nodded. She understood that.

"I went to Waikura with a guy who reckoned he wanted to look after me. I thought, this is my ticket to a real life, a decent life." She gave a bitter little laugh.

"It...didn't work out?"

"A free servant was all he wanted, really. And sex on tap. I was so grateful for a roof over my head and three meals a day—even meals I had to cook my-self—that I let him have anything he wanted, did every-thing he told me to. It got to be such a habit that after the baby came and he…wanted me to 'earn our keep,' I went back to doing the only thing I'd ever learned to do well.''

Alysia was appalled. How disillusioned she must have been.

Rita took a deep breath. ''I drank to take my mind off what I was doing. And I discovered that living that way in Waikura was even worse than in Auck-land.''

Alysia believed her. In a city people could live anonymous lives. Waikura wasn't big enough for that.

''Every time I went to a movie, or even out shop-ping,'' Rita said, ''I'd be bumping in to men who…who knew me. Most of them pretended they didn't. The others…'' She stooped to pick up a bro-ken shell, absently brushing sand off it as they walked, her head bent as though the task was impor-tant and absorbing. ''I don't know which was worse, having them smirk at me or having them look through me. But too many people knew. When I realized why my little boy was always coming home from school with bruises or a bloodied nose, I had to do some-thing.''

She closed her fist on the shell and then stopped briefly, hurling it toward the water. ''Started by trying to beat the drink. I met Graeme at an AA meeting. He'd gone bankrupt because of his drinking. We helped each other, and I realized I didn't have to live without self-respect, without the respect of my own son.''

''I'm sure you have that.''

"Maybe now. I hope so." Rita drew a deep breath. "But I'm not sure what those years did to him. I worried about him going back to that place. He can't have been happy there. Why pick Waikura, of all places?"

Alysia was silent, recalling Hurley saying to Chase, "You always said, *I'll show you.*"

So he'd returned to the town that had despised him to show that he could be someone, that he wasn't to be looked down on anymore. He'd got the unofficial king of Waikura to make him one of the family, give him half the kingdom and his daughter's hand.

"Maybe," Alysia said, "he had something to prove." Was that better than naked ambition for its own sake?

Rita said, "I just wanted to tell you my side. There might be people who remember and...it must be hard for a girl like you to understand how Chase comes to have a mother like me."

"I think he's very lucky to have a mother like you," Alysia said with utter sincerity as the two men turned and waited for them to catch up.

It had taken courage and determination for Rita to overcome her early background and her teenage mistakes, and to bring up a son who hadn't ended up on the wrong side of the law.

"What a lovely thing to say!" Impulsively Rita threw her arms about Alysia and hugged her.

In the spare bedroom later, Chase asked, "What was my mother being so...effusive about down on the beach?"

Alysia slipped under the bed covers. "I told her you were lucky to have her."

He was hanging up a pair of trousers. Closing the wardrobe door, he turned. "You always know the right thing to say, don't you, Princess?"

Alysia swallowed anger. "I wasn't just saying the right thing. She beat a drinking problem and turned her life around. For *your* sake. Don't you admire her for that?"

Chase came over to the bed and got in beside her. "Sure I do. I'm proud of my mother. She's earned my respect as well as my love. But I don't expect you to feel the same way."

He had never expected very much of her at all, Alysia thought bleakly. Least of all that she show the kind of strength and courage his mother had. She switched off the bedside light. "You have no idea how lucky you are."

When they arrived back in Waikura Aunt Patricia departed for Auckland, and Alysia took over caring for her father and the house, not returning to the *Clarion* office.

Chase was surprised. "What will you do?"

"It's a big house. And it'll take more looking after now that Dad's home all day and there are three of us living here."

"You want to be a housewife?"

"What else would you suggest?"

Chase gave her a baffled look. "I thought you might want to take over some of the business side at the *Clarion*. We work well together..."

She was damned if she was going to take a place made for her by grace and favor of her husband. A place secondary to his position as the new king of the castle. Rubbing salt into wounds that were still raw.

"No, thanks. It's all yours—as long as you stay married to me."

"Till death us do part." He paused. "You don't doubt that, do you?"

"How could I? You've got everything you wanted, haven't you?"

Frowning, he said slowly, "I wanted *you*, Alysia. What did you want?"

"Nothing." Her smile was dazzling. "Nothing but you. I'm the happiest woman in the world."

Spencer didn't grow any roses. Instead he decided to write a history of the *Clarion*. Alysia became his unofficial assistant, looking up references for him in the *Clarion's* library, fetching clippings or photographs, interviewing old employees on his behalf.

Visiting the *Clarion* offices to collect some material that Glenys had gathered for the history, Alysia fancied that the secretary was disappointed Spencer hadn't called for them himself.

"Dad's a bit down this week," Alysia explained. "Why don't you come to dinner tonight? You haven't been around for a while and you'd cheer him up."

"I doubt it," Glenys said rather snappily.

Alysia stared, and the older woman flushed.

"Did you have a disagreement?" Alysia asked. "His illness makes him a bit...testy sometimes."

Glenys laughed. "Alysia, your father's always been a bit testy!" It was the first criticism of Spencer that Alysia had ever heard pass his ex-secretary's lips. But she recognized the note of tolerant affection that softened the words.

"I think he's missing you."

Glenys shook her head. "The only woman he's ever really missed is your mother."

Alysia said gently, "She's been gone a long time now. You've brought him a great deal of...comfort." Hearing herself, she said apologetically, "But I suppose he hasn't given you much in return."

"Oh, that's not true! Your father is a very generous man, a very...loving man, in his way," Glenys finished wistfully. "It's just that I want more than he can give me."

Don't I know the feeling, Alysia thought, her heart hollow. How many years had this poor woman wasted on a man who felt only a lukewarm affection for her? "You've broken off with him?"

"I suggested we should both...consider our position, now that he's left the newspaper and you are married." She smiled cheerlessly. "He just said that of course I must do whatever I thought was best for me. In the same tone he used to say, 'Send a memo.' Well, that put me well and truly in my place! I've never been more to him than an accommodating secretary...with extended duties."

"Did you know," Alysia said diffidently, "he feels that his illness has made him less...um...virile?"

Glenys blinked. Then her eyes widened in comprehension. "He thinks that would make a difference to me?"

"I wouldn't be surprised."

Glenys looked at her with doubt that turned to dawning hope, then a softness that caught at Alysia's heart. "Oh, no! The poor dear! Men are so sensitive about that sort of thing."

"He should have told you."

"Yes, he should." Glenys seemed to brace herself

and come to a decision. "I...I might come to dinner after all, if the invitation is still open?"

Alysia stopped on the way out to use the staff ladies' room. As she was washing her hands a young girl rushed in, entered a cubicle and noisily locked the door behind her. But the flimsy partition didn't stop the sound of stifled sobbing coming through.

Alysia dried her hands and lingered, unwilling to leave someone in such distress.

Eventually the sobs abated and the door opened. The girl looked ready to bolt back into the cubicle, but Alysia smiled and said, "Hello, Franny."

"Hello." Cautiously she emerged, not meeting Alysia's eyes. She bent over a basin and dashed cold water over her swollen eyes and blotched face.

Alysia handed her a paper towel.

"Thanks." Her voice muffled, she dried her face and then looked in the mirror. "O—oh!"

"What's happened?" Alysia asked quietly.

Franny slid her a doubtful glance. "N-nothing, really. I'm being silly."

"You were very upset. Can I help?"

Franny started to cry again. "You won't believe me. No one will!"

"Try me," Alysia suggested.

The girl shook her head vehemently, then wiped her eyes with the paper towel, her mouth turning down. "You're Mr. Osborne's wife."

"So?"

"So...he'd take Mr. Hastie's side, of course."

Alysia felt a cold shiver start at the top of her head and ripple down her spine. "Mr. Hastie?"

"I never said anything!"

"What did he do?" Alysia asked calmly, her whole being in a state of suspension. "He touched you, didn't he? Tried to make you touch him?"

Franny's mouth opened, her eyes wide and scared. "How did you know?"

"Is this the first time?" Alysia asked her.

The girl looked away. "He's been trying for months to get me to...and he's right, why would anyone believe me when he's been working here for donkey's years? He's on town committees and everything. They're not going to do anything to *him*, are they? The paper couldn't run without him. They'd sack me, not him!"

Alysia clamped her teeth on a wave of nausea. "No, they won't," she said grimly. "How old are you?"

"Sixteen. I just left school last year. I love this job, I really want to learn about printing." Her shoulders sagged. "I can't stand it anymore. But I'd never get another job in Waikura. And I hate Auckland." Her lips trembled. "What'll I do?"

Alysia said decisively, "You are coming with me."

"Where?" Franny asked apprehensively.

"To see my...your boss."

"Mr. Osborne? No—" Frantically the girl shook her head.

"Yes," Alysia said, taking her arm. "Don't worry. He'll listen." She would make damned sure he did.

"But..." Franny's eyes glazed over with, Alysia thought, sheer terror. It kept her quiet until Alysia had her in Chase's office, sweeping past a surprised Glenys with a brief word and flinging open the door.

She closed it behind them and faced her husband across the desk as he rose to his feet.

"Sit down, Franny," Alysia said, pushing her into a chair. Her hand resting protectively on the girl's shoulder, she told Chase, "I made Franny come. She has something to tell you."

The girl made a choked little sound, and Alysia said, "It's okay. Just tell us what's been going on."

Once Franny began it all came out in a rush, and when she had finished she sat twisting the damp paper towel she still clutched.

Chase sank back in his chair, staring at her, then at Alysia. Frowning, he passed a hand over his hair. "Franny," he said, "do you have proof of any of this? Any witnesses?"

Miserably the girl said, "I knew you wouldn't believe me!"

"I didn't say that," Chase said evenly. "Only when it's your word against Verne's, with nothing else to go on...well, I'm not sure there's enough evidence to act on."

"Why should she make up something like this?" Alysia demanded. "You can see how distressed she is!"

Chase looked at her sharply, then back at Franny, who had begun crying again. "Have you mentioned this to anyone else?" he asked her.

Sobbing, she shook her head.

"Franny," he said gently, "I'm sending you home."

"I knew you'd give me the sack!" she wailed.

Alysia said, "Chase! You can't—"

"I'm not sacking you," he assured Franny, cutting across Alysia's protest. "You're upset and I want you to go home, calm down and try not to worry about this while I talk to Verne." He pressed a button on his phone and said, "Glenys, can you come in here, please?" Then he came around the desk and helped Franny to her feet. "I'll be in touch. Would you mind not talking to your family about it, meantime?"

Franny wiped her eyes again and nodded. "I'll say I felt sick."

Chase asked Glenys to drive her home, and if the secretary was surprised she didn't show it, guiding the tearful girl out with an arm about her shoulders.

As soon as the door closed Alysia turned on Chase. "Are you going to let it go?"

"I'm going to talk to Verne," he said.

"He'll deny it. And that'll be the end of it. Except that an innocent girl will lose her job."

"You heard me tell her—"

"That you won't sack her? Do you think she'll be able to keep working here? You saw the state that man's reduced her to. And he'll go on as though nothing ever happened."

"I can't ruin a man's life and career on the strength of one accusation that can't be corroborated. At the moment I'm inclined to believe at least that Franny has received unwelcome attention—"

"Sexual harassment!"

"But she hasn't suggested he raped her."

"Oh, so if he didn't actually *rape* her that's all right?"

"It's a very serious charge and I will certainly investigate it. But even if it's true, as this is the first time—"

"It isn't the first time."

"What?" Chase's eyes became alert and questioning.

"It isn't the first time he's done this."

"Are you sure of your facts?"

"I'm as sure as anyone can be."

"How?" he shot at her. "You've never mentioned this before."

"No, I haven't. But Verne Hastie did the same kind of thing to me...when I was only fourteen years old."

Chapter Twelve

"He *what?*" Chase rose from his chair, his cheeks
sallow.

"If Franny wants to take this further, I'll offer to
give evidence."

"Didn't you tell your father?" Chase demanded.

"Yes." Alysia was unable to go on. She looked
beyond him, remembering the humiliation and hurt.

"*Alysia?*" Chase's voice brought her back. "What
happened?"

"Verne said...I was asking for it."

Chase made a deep, guttural sound.

Forcing her eyes to meet his, she went on. "I'd
made the mistake of saying I was going to tell. But
before I'd plucked up the courage to complain to my
father Verne got in first with his version."

"What version?"

"That I had a crush on him, that I'd been hanging
around him for weeks, trying to get him to...kiss me,
touch me. He said he'd told me not to be a silly little

girl and out of spite I'd threatened to say he'd molested me.'' She had to steady her voice. "So my father said I wasn't to come here anymore. I made too much trouble for the staff.''

Chase's voice grated. "He didn't believe you?''

"If he'd believed me he'd have had to find a new print manager, wouldn't he?''

"Alysia, I'm sure that wasn't—''

"It had to be a consideration,'' she said. "Nothing is as important to him as the newspaper. You know that.''

"You're his daughter!''

Alysia gave him a twisted little smile. After a moment she said, "He never told you, did he?''

"About this business with Verne? No—it's the first I've heard of it.''

That wasn't what she'd meant, but maybe this was not the right time. "What are you going to do about Verne?''

He was looking at her with a puzzled expression. "Have him in here, ask some questions. Then decide.''

Alysia turned to leave. "You do that.''

Her father was in the hall when she got home.

"You're back,'' he said.

"Yes.'' Alysia handed over the package. "Glenys says she hopes this is everything you asked for.''

Spencer cleared his throat. "How is she?'' He looked, for him, very nearly anxious.

"You'll see for yourself. I invited her to dinner.''

"And she accepted?'' Was that hope she saw in his face? But the scowl that succeeded it was unmistakable.

"You've missed her, haven't you?"

"Hmph." Spencer looked down at the sheaf of papers in his hands. "I have work to do on these," he muttered, and stumped off to his study.

Chase was late coming home, and as soon as she heard the car Alysia hurried into the kitchen to begin dishing up the meal.

The atmosphere between her father and their guest was so tense that Glenys had uncharacteristically downed three glasses of white wine in rapid succession, probably on an empty stomach, and was looking flushed and nervous. It would be a kindness to feed her. Besides, Alysia acknowledged to herself, she'd been glad to escape. The strain was telling on her, too.

She put the glazed lamb in the microwave to reheat, then poured potatoes into a dish, nearly dropping it as she turned and found Chase standing in her way.

He rescued the dish and placed it on the worktable.

"I didn't hear you come in."

"Sorry I'm late. I've made my apologies to Spencer and Glenys. What's going on there? They're like a couple of cats on hot bricks."

"They have things to sort out," Alysia said vaguely. "Where have you been?"

"I went to see Franny." He leaned back against the table, folding his arms.

"Did you pay her off?"

"What?"

"Did you offer her a few hundred dollars and tell her not to come back to work?"

Chase's eyes narrowed. "No." He paused. "I told her Verne had been warned—"

"Oh—you *warned* him?" Alysia's voice was filled with mock awe. "That must have scared him silly!"

"I hope it did," Chase said grimly. "Much as I'd like to, I can't sack a man out of hand for an offence that hasn't been proven in any court. He'd be entitled to bring a case for wrongful dismissal."

"If I testify—"

Chase shook his head. "Franny is adamant about not involving the police, and we can't force her. But I told Verne if there are any more complaints from her or anyone else I'll encourage her to take it further and back her all the way."

"You did?" Alysia said blankly.

"And gave him three months to find another job where there are no young women. I won't give him a reference if there are."

Alysia had trouble taking it in. "Thank you," she said, dazed. It was silly, she supposed, but the rush of relief she felt was like cool spring water on a long-time ache.

At last someone believed her. *Chase* believed her. She said, "It's about time someone called his bluff."

"I've offered Franny a transfer to another department if she wants it, but made it clear she's entitled to remain where she is if she prefers the work. If she has any more problems she's to come straight to me and I'll deal with it. If there's ever a next time Verne's out on his ear. No matter what. I'll deal with any flak after the fact."

Alysia felt almost dizzy. "I thought..."

"That I'd be on his side?" Chase's mouth moved in a wry grimace. "I thought of him putting his dirty hands on you when you were only a child, and I wanted to kill him. But I had to handle this profes-

sionally, not on a personal level. Once he gives me
the slightest excuse I'll have him out of there so fast
his feet won't touch the ground.''

''My father says he's a very good print manager—
one of the best.''

Chase looked at her strangely. ''Did you actually
believe I wouldn't do anything about this because the
man is good at his work?''

''It's how my father handled it.''

Chase frowned. ''I don't understand that.'' He
straightened and put his hands on her arms, pulling
her toward him. ''It can't have been long after you'd
lost your mother.''

''Less than a year.''

Chase's fingers tightened. His voice quiet but coming from between his teeth, he said, ''And Verne...
the bloody pervert.''

''My father won't approve of you telling him to
find another job.''

''Spencer isn't in charge anymore. I am.''

The microwave oven beeped, and she tugged away
from him to take out the lamb.

He was watching her. ''That's why you kept away
from the *Clarion* offices during the holidays,'' he
said. ''I thought you weren't interested.''

She put the meat on the table and picked up a couple of spring onions, carefully arranging them to gar-
nish the dish. ''I never said I wasn't interested.''

''But when I asked if you'd taken journalism to
please your father you didn't deny it.''

Alysia's shoulder lifted.

''You'd do anything for him, wouldn't you?''
Chase said slowly. ''Have you ever done a single
thing because it was what *you* wanted? Do you really

think your father expects you to be some kind of bond-slave?''

Alysia stared down at the surface of the table without really seeing anything. ''You don't understand.''

''No, I don't. I hoped once we were married I'd be able to get under that glossy surface, find the real you that I'd caught a glimpse of now and then. But that…veneer of yours just got shinier and more slippery every day. Until this afternoon, when you brought Franny in and got so angry with me.''

''I'm sorry. I jumped to conclusions and I shouldn't have.''

He brushed that away with an impatient movement of his hand. ''At least the anger was real.''

''I thought you were going to sweep the whole thing under the carpet. My father's going to be furious that it's out in the open. Especially at you giving Verne the sack.''

He came to stand behind her, and she saw them reflected in the window, saw him looking baffled but purposeful. ''Alysia—I keep Spencer informed about what goes on at the paper and listen to his opinion because I value his experience, and because it's important for him not to feel totally cut off now that he's handed the paper over to me. But I'm not his puppet.''

''I know that,'' Alysia said, her lips twisting in a painful smile. ''It was you pulling the strings all along, wasn't it? He thinks it was him, but you got what you wanted. Do you always?''

Chase put his hands on her shoulders, made her face him. His eyes were intent and serious, a frown between the straight brows. ''What do you think I wanted, Alysia?''

"Control of the paper. Ownership."

"I don't own the *Clarion*—it's in trust for our children."

"*Your* children. Not my children by anyone else."

"You're married to me! Were you thinking of having a family with someone else?"

"You know what I mean!"

"I'm beginning to think I do," Chase agreed grimly. "Spencer was protecting your interests—"

Alysia shook her head. "He was protecting the *Clarion*. Don't you realize yet why he was so keen for us to get married? It was the only way he could pass the paper on to you without any apparent unfairness to me."

"You wanted the *Clarion?*"

She shrugged out of his hold and walked across the room to the stove, lifting a pot of green beans to shake them into a serving dish. "Kingsleys have always owned it and run it, since Jasper Kingsley printed the first issue two years after he founded the town. I trained—educated myself—to be ready when it was my turn."

"I suppose Spencer was afraid there wouldn't be time," Chase said. "You were too inexperienced to take over if he were to die in the near future."

"He didn't have to give it away!" she cried, banging the empty pot down on the stove and swinging around again.

Chase studied the resentment in her face and said quietly, "No, and I don't suppose he realized how much it meant to you. *I* certainly hadn't." He drew in a deep breath. "You've been jealous of me all along, haven't you? That's why you were so prickly when he made me his deputy."

Alysia swallowed hard and remained silent. Because he was right. She'd seen the writing on the wall, known that Chase was being groomed to take over, that her own position as Spencer Kingsley's daughter was under threat.

"Alysia—why did you marry me?"

The question was so unexpected that she stared at him while it penetrated. But she wasn't ready to throw her pride in the dust. It was all she had left. Everything else had been taken from her. "For the same reason you married me. Don't think I'm complaining. I knew what the deal was and I went along with it."

"Why?" Chase demanded again. "You knew the night before the wedding that Spencer had taken the *Clarion* from you. You could have called the marriage off."

"Don't imagine I wasn't tempted. Habit, I suppose." Not for anything would she tell him that she'd been desperately, head over heels in love with him. So much so that the thought of not being with him, of not sharing his life, had terrified her even more than the bitter knowledge that he'd married her for reasons that had nothing to do with the kind of searing, overwhelming emotions she felt for him. "You just said, I've always done what my father wanted."

Chase paled. "That is not a reason!"

"It's as good as any," Alysia said indifferently. "And I didn't mind… I can't say it's any hardship, being your wife." She gave him a slanting, ironic smile, trying to sound uncaring. "And my father got the son he never had by marrying him to the daughter he's never wanted."

Chase blinked. "Who told you he never wanted you?"

"You still don't know, do you?" Alysia's smile widened until it hurt, because if she didn't smile she was going to burst into tears. "You should have put a pea under the mattress on our wedding night—then maybe you'd have known."

"A *pea?*"

Her laughter was shaky, then the smile abruptly faded. Willing her lips not to tremble, her voice to remain steady, she said flippantly, "You must know the old fairy tale—it's the test of a true princess. My father cheated you, I'm afraid. I'm not really his daughter at all."

Chapter Thirteen

"**Y**ou're not Spencer's daughter?" Chase looked baffled.

"He and my mother adopted me as a baby."

At first Chase didn't react at all. Then he looked at her with an odd expression on his face that she failed to interpret. "You're adopted. So what?" he said flatly. "Was it legal?"

"Oh, yes. Signed papers, birth certificate and every-thing."

"Then surely that's as real as it gets. They call adoptees 'chosen children.' It's a very deliberate act, adopting a baby. Why should you think," Chase asked carefully, "that you weren't wanted?"

"I always knew it deep down. And my aunt talked about…things. I pieced together quite a lot."

"Like what?"

"Like…there seemed no reason why my parents couldn't have children, but they'd been married for seven years and had none. My mother wanted to adopt and she talked my...my father into it. She told him some of those stories about people who adopt and nine months later have a natural child. It happens.''

He nodded. ''So I've heard.''

''Well, according to Aunt Patricia, my father agreed on condition they adopted a girl.''

Chase briefly rubbed his chin, a line appearing between his brows. ''I think I see,'' he said quietly.

''They did have a son, years later. The first and last child my mother ever conceived.''

Chase looked puzzled. ''But you don't have a brother.'' He paused. ''Do you?''

''It was a stillbirth. The baby never breathed.''

Then the door was pushed wider and Glenys was there, smiling in a rather strained way and asking, ''Can I help, Alysia?''

''Yes,'' Alysia accepted. ''Things are getting cold.'' She thrust the dish of beans into Chase's hands and gave the potatoes to Glenys. ''Take these through. I'll bring the rest.''

It wasn't a particularly comfortable meal. Chase and Spencer both appeared to be thinking of something else, and the women's valiant efforts at conversation went largely unregarded. Alysia was serving dessert when Spencer finally roused himself. ''Tell me what's been happening down at the office,'' he demanded, his imperious gaze going from Glenys to Chase.

''Nothing much,'' Chase said, unusually taciturn.

Glenys, Alysia was sure, would normally have followed her new boss's discreet lead. But she'd continued to make inroads on the wine that Alysia had

served with dinner, and it showed. Someone would
have to drive her home.

"What are you going to do about that poor little
girl?" Glenys asked Chase. "She was in a terrible
state when I took her home."

"What girl?" Spencer looked up from his plate.

"Franny from the print room."

Chase asked quickly, "What did she say to you?"

Glenys seemed to realize she'd let her customary
discretion slip. "Not much," she said guiltily.
"You'd told her not to talk about it. But I guessed. I
must say, I've sometimes wondered about Verne Hastie."

"Wondered?" Spencer scowled at her.

"There was a high turnover of young females in
the print department. It seemed odd, in a place like
Waikura where jobs are hard to come by."

"Verne said they found the work too heavy and
noisy," Spencer offered shortly.

Chase gave him a steady look. "Franny says he
sexually assaulted her."

Spencer looked stunned. "No one ever complained."

Alysia's head buzzed. She pushed away her half-
emptied plate, unable to look at anyone.

She heard Chase's voice. "Alysia did—didn't
she?"

Glenys sounded shocked. *"When?"*

Lifting her head, Alysia was aware of a dull surprise. Glenys knew everything that went on at the
Clarion, but she supposed her father had regarded the
incident as a family matter. And in all these years he
had never mentioned it to the woman he was so close
to.

"There was no corroboration," Spencer said.

"Only Alysia's word." There was a hard edge in Chase's voice. "Wasn't that good enough?"

Alysia stirred, ready to leave the table, but her husband's hand shot out and closed over hers, holding her there. "Now you know she wasn't the only one. I think you owe her an apology, don't you?" he challenged Spencer.

Spencer looked affronted.

Alysia said hurriedly, "There's no need."

Her father's expression changed. He passed a hand over his eyes. "You have to understand," he said almost pleading with her. "You'd lost your mother, and I—" he cleared his throat "—I had never been a very active parent. Didn't know anything about teenage girls."

"It's all right," she assured him. Seeing him so unsure of himself was a revelation, and it made her uncomfortable.

Spencer didn't seem to be listening. "Verne had daughters of his own. He was still quite good-looking then...and he was all sympathy and understanding. He told me that after losing your mother you were needing affection, and it was natural to turn to someone older, but because you were just hitting puberty you'd muddled affection and...and sex. He didn't blame you at all, but he was concerned that someone less scrupulous might take advantage of you, because the way you were acting was..."

"Asking for it," Alysia whispered, feeling sick. She took a harsh, shaken breath.

"It was very plausible, especially since I'd been making a pretty bad fist of trying to provide you with all that was missing in your life." Spencer said heavily, "We both lost a great deal when your mother went. You're a good girl, and she would have been proud of you."

A tight band that had been constricting her heart for so long that she hadn't realized it was there seemed to loosen a trifle. "I know you did your best for me," she said quietly.

Chase seemed about to speak but Glenys forestalled him. "That's an excuse, Spencer," she said, as though reminding him of a forgotten appointment, "not an apology."

All of them looked at her in surprise. She sat ramrod straight, watching Spencer bravely.

Spencer looked as if a mouse had suddenly bitten his ankle.

"It doesn't matter—" Alysia started.

Spencer stopped staring at Glenys, and slowly turned to Alysia, almost as if he didn't believe what he was doing. "I'm sorry," he said simply. And then, his expression changing to one of genuine sorrow, perhaps released by the words, "My dear girl—I'm so very sorry."

"It's all right," Alysia repeated, more strongly than before. Tears pricked at her eyes, and her throat was raw. The hard band loosened further. "It's really all right, Dad."

Glenys helped Alysia clear the table, urging Chase to keep Spencer company while the women made coffee. "I think I need it," she confessed to Alysia. Her eyes were bright and she was still flushed, but she carried a pile of dishes and deposited them on the counter above the dishwasher. "Only I hope I haven't run out of Dutch courage quite yet."

Alysia gave her a rather bewildered smile, reaching for the coffee filter. "What do you need more for?"

"I decided before I came that tonight I was going to have it out with your father. I hope that we'll get some time alone before I leave. I mean...more than a few minutes. I'm sorry if that's rude—"

"Not at all. I'll see to it," Alysia promised.

"I'm going to make him tell me what's wrong, and I'll make it clear I don't give a damn, except for the sake of his silly old pride." A shadow of doubt clouded Glenys's eyes. "I'm gambling on his feelings for me. Because sometimes, you know, I've thought he does love me in his funny, reticent way."

"I'm certain you're right."

Glenys nodded. "But I'm not going to be treated like a shameful secret any longer. He either regularizes the situation or..." She swallowed. "If he can't accord me the respect that I deserve, then I'm better off without him."

Chase took the hint when Alysia said she was sure Glenys would excuse them if they left her with Spencer. Declining the older man's almost panicky invitation to stay, he followed Alysia upstairs.

"She'd better not drive home," he said as they reached the bedroom.

"I made her promise to call a cab," Alysia said. "If she goes home."

Chase cocked a curious eyebrow, but Alysia said no more. She got her silver robe and went straight to the bathroom for a long, soothing shower, easing away tensions. When she came back Chase had loosened his shirt all the way and pulled it from his pants.

He was standing by the window with his hands in the pockets of his dark trousers.

"Sorry," she said. "Did I take too long?"

"It's okay." He turned, toward the bathroom, she thought, but as they passed he reached out and snagged her wrist in his long fingers.

"What is it?"

His eyes were grave and searching. "Alysia, being adopted doesn't mean your father doesn't love you. And it doesn't obligate you, either. Whatever his motives, he volunteered for the job of father. You don't have to spend your life being grateful."

Alysia looked down, biting her lower lip. "Isn't it funny," she mused, "how universal truths never penetrate until they become personal?"

"What do you mean?"

"You can't buy love after all, can you? And you can't force it, either."

"No."

"I suppose...we've made our bed, you and I. Now we have no choice but to lie on it."

He looked at her for a long, silent moment, his eyes shadowed and dark. "There is a choice." His voice had gone hard again. "If you want to make it."

"If I...?"

"It's up to you, Alysia. For once in your life do something for yourself." He paused as she looked blankly at him, then said, forcing the words out, "Anytime you want a divorce—it's yours."

"Divorce?" Mentally reeling, Alysia stared at him. "But..." Didn't he understand what a divorce would mean to his future plans, to everything he'd worked toward for years? "You'd lose the *Clarion!*" Spencer had made it perfectly clear that Chase's position depended on him being married to her.

Momentarily Chase closed his eyes. When he opened them again they were blazing. She realized that for some reason he was quietly but consumingly furious. "*For God's sake!* If you'd wake up out of that pathetic fairy tale you seem to live in it might occur to you that not everyone feels the world begins and ends at Waikura—and that running a provincial daily isn't the pinnacle of success!"

Dazed and bewildered, she protested, "But you wanted it! You wanted to show Waikura you could be someone!"

"What the hell makes you think that?"

"Why else would you have come back and stayed so long? Why else would you have married me?"

She thought he wanted to yell at her. He took a moment to moderate his voice to a controlled vehemence. "Do you really think I married you to gain control of your father's piddling little paper?"

As Alysia continued to stare at him he said, "You do, don't you? Though *why* you should think so is beyond my comprehension." He took a deep breath. "I came back because there was a job going here, and—" he paused "—maybe deep down, yes, I might have relished the chance to show Waikura what I was made of, that I was as good as anyone else in this narrow-minded town. I stayed because I was advancing up the career ladder faster than I could have on a bigger paper. And I figured I owed Spencer another year or two before moving on. Then you came home, and Spencer had a heart attack, and…things got complicated."

"Because he was pushing you into marriage with me."

"Because I was falling in love with you," Chase said fiercely. "And Spencer was throwing you into my arms. I knew you didn't have a clue what the hell you were doing. You were too damned young and you'd been too protected to have any idea what love is."

Alysia studied him with wide eyes, afraid to blink in case this was a dream and she might be awake when she opened them again. If this was true, then she'd been wildly, perhaps unforgivably wrong about his motives, his feelings. And she owed it to him to be honest. She owed it to herself, and their marriage. She swallowed, touched her tongue to her lips and said steadily, "I do know what love is, Chase."

"You do?" Clearly he doubted it.

"You just said...you were falling in love with me?"

His mouth twisted. "Don't worry about that. I'll survive. Somehow."

"You never said you loved me until the night before our wedding," she accused, "when you were afraid I might call it off." When, she'd thought, he knew she'd been shocked at her father's plans and was prepared to say anything to stop her from wrecking them.

"I may have taken shameless advantage of your naiveté and your need for your father's approval," he said, "but I'm not totally without principles. I wasn't going to compound matters by making you feel guilty for not being able to love me."

"How...how do you know I don't?"

"Don't tease, Alysia," he said hoarsely. "The time

for that is way past. And if you want that divorce let me know soon, because I don't think I could stand being kept in suspense for too long."

"But—"

He wasn't listening, he'd turned on his heel and was walking into the bathroom. Even as she tried to speak, he'd banged the door behind him.

When he emerged, his hair damp and tousled, a towel tucked about his waist, and a faint wisp of steam following him, Alysia was standing exactly where he'd left her. Almost as soon as the door opened, she said, "I don't want a divorce."

Chase stopped in midstride and closed his eyes. He seemed to sway a little on his feet.

When he looked at her his eyes were watchful and, she thought, deliberately enigmatic. "You'd better be sure," he said. "I may not give you a chance to change your mind. Do you want to think about it?"

"I don't need to. I lied to you, Chase...about why I married you." She'd had a few minutes to think, to absorb what he was trying to tell her, to unlock the guard she'd put on her heart at the beginning of their marriage, and to work up the courage to speak her mind. This was no time to wrap her feelings in wary cynicism or pretend she didn't care, trying to protect herself against being hurt again. If Chase loved her, there was nothing to be afraid of. "I lay awake all night before our wedding day," she told him, "trying to imagine leaving you at the altar, living without you, and I couldn't bear it. I wanted to hate you. I'd just seen my father give you everything I thought should have been mine, and I was eaten up with jealousy and hurt. But I still wanted you...loved you."

"You love me?" Chase looked dazed, taking a hesitant step toward her.

Shamed by her lack of trust, her heart aching at the dawning hope replacing disbelief on his face, she confessed, "I can't seem to help it."

He swooped then and gathered her close, holding her tightly with his cheek warming hers. "Oh, God!" he breathed against her skin. "I was so scared that you'd tell me to go, that you'd want to rid yourself of me."

"If I hadn't loved you so much I would never have agreed to the marriage." She had her arms about his neck, and her voice was muffled against his shirt. "I'd do a lot for my father but I'm not prepared to throw away my whole life to please him. Only I thought that you…"

He eased himself away and held her shoulders. "You thought I was willing to take you as part of the bargain, to get my hands on the *Clarion*." He shook his head. "How could you love a man like that?"

"It didn't seem to make any difference," she admitted. "But I'm glad you're not that kind of man. Chase, I'm so sorry. You have every right to be angry and insulted."

"You bloody well should be sorry." He lifted her, ignoring her muffled shriek as he dumped her on the bed.

Lying beside her, he pulled at the loose knot of her belt and bent to kiss her. "I'll make you do penance for it the rest of our lives."

"Penance?"

"You have to tell me you love me every single day. And twice on Sundays."

"No problem." She kissed his cheek before he

moved away to look down at her, a slight smile curving his lips, anger apparently forgotten.

His hand ran over the satin from her waist to her shoulder, pausing along the way. "We could get your father to alter the trust, give you the blasted paper. I never really wanted it anyway."

"Never?" Her fingers drifted over his chest.

"I went along with the trust business because it came as part of the package, with you. You were what was keeping me here, not the newspaper. If it hadn't been for you, and your father's heart attack, I'd have taken an offer I had from Wellington. It was a good one. Alysia—if you want the *Clarion* I'll happily hand over to you. Spencer will have to change the damned trust if I refuse it. After all, you're legally his heir."

She could see he meant it. His eyes met hers with utter seriousness, even though his hands were occupied in deliciously distracting ways. "What would you do?"

"I'll think of something. Maybe I'll start up a rival paper, give you a run for your money." He grinned at her, an eyebrow raised in interrogation.

"In Waikura?" She looked at him with suspicion, a smile lurking on her lips.

"If this is where you're going to be. I can't leave you, Princess. You've cast a spell on me."

"Witches do that, not princesses," she said absently, and paused. "He's trapped you, hasn't he?" Dimly she realized how dreadful that was. "We don't have to let him do it! If you'd like to leave here, go on with your career elsewhere...I'll come with you."

He looked at her soberly, and said at last, "What I'd like is for us to be partners. Your business degree could be a real asset, and you're wasting it. I miss you in the office. Why didn't you want to continue after the wedding?"

"I thought you were throwing me a sop." She chewed over the idea. "If you really mean it, I think I'd like that."

Her hurt and bitterness had begun to dissipate at last. This was different from going back to the *Clarion* when she believed that Chase had married her because Spencer had used the paper as bait. This was Chase offering an equal partnership. Not some sinecure to keep the little woman happy. "But is the *Clarion* really what you want?"

"When and if the time comes for a change, we'll make sure your inheritance is in good hands."

"Neither of us has roots here, really, do we?" Alysia mused. "I don't know where I came from. And my father is the last of the Kingsleys."

He looked up at the ceiling and then returned a thoughtful gaze to her. "We could give the name to our children."

"You wouldn't mind?"

"I don't know my real father's name," he said. "I took my stepfather's because it was convenient to have the same name as my mother. I'll change it again to yours if you'd like that."

If he had made such a suggestion earlier it would have confirmed her mistaken beliefs about him, hardened her jealousy and insecurity. Now she just smiled and shook her head. "My father would love that, but it doesn't matter to me. I was never a Kingsley by birth, and it's not important anymore."

They lay quietly, his hand stroking her arm, her fingers splayed on his chest, feeling the beating of his heart, and for the first time in months she felt drowsily content. "I wonder how Glenys is getting on. I think she was going to make Dad propose."

"Make him...?" Chase's skepticism dissolved into quiet laughter. "She might, too. I've never seen her so aggressive."

"Not aggressive—assertive. You think he will?"

Chase rolled onto his back, staring at the ceiling for a second or two, then propped himself on his elbow, looking down at her, his fingers playing with her hair, separating the strands. "He's a fool if he doesn't. She'll persuade him. I have some experience of Glenys's subtle methods." He picked up Alysia's hand and began kissing the knuckles, then the inside of her wrist.

Alysia smiled at the top of his dark head. "Chase...?"

"Yes, my darling?" His hand caressed her inner arm and slid over the satin that covered her breasts, and pushed the edges of the gown apart. "God, you're beautiful!"

His mouth covered hers, and they exchanged a long, sweet kiss while his hands did wonderful things to her, thrusting the impeding gown out of the way. Everywhere he touched tiny flames were licking over her, until her entire body was alight. She pressed closer to him, slipping her thigh between his, wanting to kindle the fire within him in return. He groaned, and she tugged at the towel round his waist, removing it with his eager cooperation.

"I want you now," she whispered, and he gave her a look of dazed enquiry. "Now," she repeated. "Please."

He needed no more pleading. She felt him glide

into her and sighed with satisfaction. Her eyelids fluttered down; her legs snugly enclosed him, welcoming him for the first time without reservation, with no residual bitterness to cloud the moment, letting herself go with him in utter trust and faith into the dark dimension of pleasure, unmixed with pain.

When he lifted his head at last she was breathless and flushed, her arms still hooked loosely about his neck, her eyes naked in love.

"You don't mind," she asked him softly, as his breathing slowed, "that I'm not a real princess?"

"You are to me," he answered, and bent to feather kisses across her skin, making her shudder with delight. "You always will be. The princess who married the peasant, and made him happy ever after."

* * * * *

King Philippe has died, leaving no male heirs to ascend the throne. Until his mother announces that a son *may* exist, embarking everyone on a desperate search for... the missing heir.

Their quest begins March 2002 and continues through June 2002.

On sale March 2002, the emotional
OF ROYAL BLOOD
by Carolyn Zane (SR #1576)

On sale April 2002, the intense
IN PURSUIT OF A PRINCESS
by Donna Clayton (SR #1582)

On sale May 2002, the heartwarming
A PRINCESS IN WAITING
by Carol Grace (SR #1588)

On sale June 2002, the exhilarating
A PRINCE AT LAST!
by Cathie Linz (SR #1594)

Available at your favorite retail outlet.

This Mother's Day
Give Your Mom
 # A Royal Treat

Win a fabulous one-week vacation in
Puerto Rico for you and your mother at
the luxurious Inter-Continental San Juan
Resort & Casino. The prize includes round
trip airfare for two, breakfast daily and a
mother and daughter day of beauty
at the beachfront hotel's spa.

INTER·CONTINENTAL
San Juan
RESORT & CASINO

Here's all you have to do:

Tell us in 100 words or less how your
mother helped with the romance in your
life. It may be a story about your engagement,
wedding or those boyfriends when you were
a teenager or any other romantic advice
from your mother. The entry will be judged
based on its originality, emotionally
compelling nature and sincerity.
See official rules on following page.

Send your entry to:
Mother's Day Contest

In Canada	**In U.S.A.**
P.O. Box 637	P.O. Box 9076
Fort Erie, Ontario	3010 Walden Ave.
L2A 5X3	Buffalo, NY
	14269-9076

Or enter online at www.eHarlequin.com

PRROY

Silhouette Romance introduces tales of
enchanted love and things beyond explanation
in the new series

Soulmates

Couples destined for each other are brought
together by the powerful magic of love....

A precious gift brings
A HUSBAND IN HER EYES
by Karen Rose Smith (on sale March 2002)

Dreams come true in
CASSIE'S COWBOY
by Diane Pershing (on sale April 2002)

A legacy of love arrives
BECAUSE OF THE RING
by Stella Bagwell (on sale May 2002)

*Available at
your favorite retail outlet.*

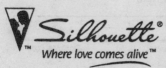

Where love comes alive™

Visit Silhouette at www.eHarlequin.com
SRSOUL